I0745471

City by the Bay Book III

Elle Klass

City by the Bay Baby Girl III

Copyright © 2014 by Elle Klass
Published 2020 Books by Elle, Inc.
ISBN: 978-1-951017-15-6
All rights reserved
Editors: Dawn Lewis
Cover art created by Manuela Cardiga
For more information go to
https://elleklass.weebly.com

Books by Elle, Inc.
225 College Dr. #65504
Orange Park, FL 32065
Booksbyelle10@gmail.com

Author's Disclaimer

This book is entirely fictional. Any characters, places or events are purely figments of the author's imagination. No part of this publication may be reproduced, transmitted or redistributed either in its entirety or in part without the author's express written consent.

Other Young Adult Books by Elle Klass

St. Augustine Novellas
Bloodseeker Series
Book 1 The Vampires Next Door
Book 2 The Monster Upstairs
Book 3 The Ghost Within

hidden journals
Isandro
Alarico

Zombie Girl
Book 1 Premonition
Book 2 Infection
Book 3 Retribution

Moonlighting in Paris Recap

Moonlighting in Paris. Cleo takes on a new identity: Justine Holmes. She travels to Paris and meets Didier, a rich hotel owner. In no time, the two become very close. She gains information on her mother's disappearance and Einstein's death. Instead of answers, she finds mystery and people who want her dead. Didier, unaware of her shaded past but well aware of her strange behavior, hires a bodyguard, Sam, to keep an eye on her.

As her and Didier's relationship peaks, a new threat appears, a warning written in lipstick, while she's working in Aruba. Justine doesn't know whether the threat is tied to her past or something in her present. Aware of the threat, unaware of her past, Sam and Didier keep her close.

Didier proposes to her. Excited, she accepts. During their engagement party her new pursuer takes the threat up a notch, attempting her harm.

Justine takes matters into her own hands, stalking her stalker. Didier's lack of knowledge about her past, and her stubborn independence, lead to the accidental death of her stalker. The guilt hanging over her head and the mystery of her birth family lead her to make a heart wrenching decision. She leaves Didier the night before the wedding, sneaking out through her terrace window, and heads home to the U.S. to solve her own family mystery.

Answers

My challenge of the day was moving through Paris undetected. I rolled my hair into a bun and wore a floppy dark green hat with a short brim over it. To further my disguise, I considered wearing heavy makeup, using bold chunks of color, but feared it would bring too much unwanted attention. I needed to blend, not stand out, so I settled for no makeup. I arrived at the airport and boarded the plane without one paparazzo chasing after me and snapping pictures. Security had been an ordeal when I showed the security agent my ID - he asked for an autograph. I leaned towards him and asked him to keep it quiet, then I signed my John Hancock, or rather Justine's. On the second flight into the U.S. a fellow passenger of male persuasion shouted, "Hey, you're Justine Holmes." Thank my goodies most passengers were sleeping.

I looked him square in the eye and said, "Nope, but thank you for the comparison." Baffled, he scrunched his brows and pinched his lips. I ignored him and he went away. The next forty-eight hours I attempted to stay hidden, with a book in front of my face, in the most vacated areas of the airport.

I purchased a last-minute flight taking me from Paris to Berlin then to Chicago. When I landed in Chicago, I wasted no time in changing my appearance and identity. I stopped at a twenty-four-hour drug store and purchased blond hair coloring and strange glasses. The glasses had thin round gold frames with tinted lenses to dull my eye color. They looked like reading glasses, but the lenses lacked magnification.

I checked into a low budget motel using cash under an assumed name. I didn't want to leave a trail. In my room I pulled an old pair of scissors I found during my dumpster diving days out of my backpack and cut my hair, which reached to my waist. After I finished chopping, it reached to the bottom of my neck, just above my shoulders. I brushed out my hair and turned my head upside down to cut leaving it with short layers. Next, I bleached it turning it an orangey yellow. I didn't look like Justine anymore. Mission accomplished.

I sat on my bed plotting out my next move and contacted my friend James, hoping to gain yet another ID, and catch up on his and LulaBell's lives. Luckily, he still lived in the motel, hiding out, using code I explained what I needed, he seemed to understand. "Got it! See you in a few days sweetie."

I planned on paying him generously for his assistance. Happy with my appearance, I left. The next few days I spent weaving around the country on busses until I reached my location. It was strange being back where I lost my love Einstein. Fear and sadness welled up in my belly, but I needed to do this.

I knocked on James' door, he opened it wide, placed his large hands on my shoulders and widened his eyes scanning me head to toe with intensity. "Wow! You have changed. I saw your picture on a magazine one day and I thought, 'I know that girl'. You're stunning even with that tangerine hair."

"It looks like a straw mop, but I don't look like the girl on that magazine, do I?"

"No, you do not!" He maneuvered his head back and forth as if to emphasis *No*. I followed him inside the room. "Justine's disappearance is going to break many a young man's heart," he said with a softness in his eyes. The crow's feet around them deeper and a few more wrinkles graced his forehead, but he still looked like James. He was the only person alive who understood anything about my woes.

"They will have to miss her. Where is LulaBell?"

"She is taking classes at the junior college. She should be home within the hour."

"College? She is only a couple years younger than me, but I can't imagine her as old enough to of graduated."

"Dual enrollment, high school classes along with college classes."

We spent the next couple hours waiting for LulaBell, catching up on our lives. I relayed my entire experience in Paris. How Halette stalked me and the nasty trick I played that started with a confrontation between her and I ending with her flipping over the railing, being carried off and thrown into a river by Mr. Dancy Eyes. I told him about Didier and leaving him at the altar because I was afraid the police would find Halette's body and trace it back to me which was partly true. I figured if I couldn't trust the man who made me a new ID every time I called, who could I trust? With all I confided in him, somehow, I still refused to discuss my search for the truth behind my birth and "kidnapping". The words in my mom's letter, Don't *ever let them find ya. They won't hestate to kill ya*, pounded in my head forcing my brain to resist any efforts to seek another soul's help in my search. However, he proved a good, confidential friend, and I needed to get most of the craziness and secrecy off my chest. He listened as I poured out my heart, once again I cried in his comforting arms. He said that Einstein's death was a big thing.

After I finished my crying bout, he handed me a beer, and we sat in the courtyard like old times. "It almost seems as though I never left," I said, sitting across the table from him and feeling as though Einstein would at any moment walk up and plop in the seat beside me, planting a kiss upon my cheek.

"Those were good times we had. Do you still cook?"

"I haven't much. There was no need Didier gave me everything. I miss it."

"You were some cook." His voice reminded me of the best time in my life when Einstein and I made a life together. "I don't want to bring up sad times for you, but how much did you learn of Einstein's death?"

"Only what I found online through papers. As much as it hurts, I want to know more."

"His family's wealthy, rich people's runaway children don't turn up dead every day. When Einstein disappeared, he was fifteen, at first the police suggested kidnapping, but no ransom request or any contact from the 'would be' kidnappers appeared. Their next possible scenario was abduction by a random pervert or killed and his body dumped. But his body never turned up anywhere. The police even suspected his parent's, but with no body there was nothing for them to pursue. Last they deduced he ran away. His parents' money and contacts made it impossible for the police and newspaper gossips to discover why."

I realized from personal experience now that money bought almost anything, even steel walls. "I am curious myself why Einstein ran away. He must've had everything. Why leave it?" I paused contemplating my words for a moment. "I had everything, and I ran away too. Money can buy a lot, but not happiness. I ran because I was in trouble, fear of a commitment to a man who really didn't know me… I told myself it wasn't fair to him. Maybe Einstein had been in trouble - something that money couldn't fix. It makes sense how he moved through homes like a ghost, understood the basics of alarms, and robbed the homeowners' blind."

James changed the flow of the conversation. "It seems you lived a privileged life in Paris."

"Yeah… I'm exhausted and turning in for the night, tell LulaBell we'll catch up later."

"Will do, night Cleo."

I paid cash up front for three days, figuring it would take at least that for my new ID to arrive. Every room looked similar and everything reminded me of Einstein, from the cheesy bed cover with vines patterned across it to the curtains. I flash-backed to the night we arrived here several years ago, how happy we both were with the simplicity of taking a hot shower. After years of living on the streets, jumping cities, stealing anything we could find of value and running innocentish scams on people to pickpocket their wallets, a hot shower and warm bed felt like a dream that night. My eyes filled with tears, I buried my head in a pillow crying myself to sleep.

The following day I contemplated everything I learned and considered what I still needed to learn compiling a short list. My mom was obviously not my real mom, but I needed to understand who she was to find my biological family - who she was hiding from, and why Slug wanted to kill a baby? To move forward I needed to work backwards. It seemed that's always what made sense.

1. find out about mom/ follow every lead

2. find real family/ be cautious

3. find out who wanted me dead/ be extremely cautious

4. Why did Elnsteln run?

My first order of business was to buy a cell phone equipped with internet and GPS with a pay-as-you-go plan. After doing so I found an internet coffee house. The unknown assailant murdered my mom at age thirty-five, which made her twenty-three when she acquired me. She wasn't in with good people, she had survival skills and street smarts, but no formal education judging by her childlike spelling and penmanship. I deduced she ran away from home.

Hundreds, thousands of children went missing daily, no shocker to me as I had fit that category myself. I didn't know where she lived as a child. I searched and searched missing children assuming my mom ran away between the ages of thirteen to sixteen, scanning the three-year window state to state.

Nothing. Nothing fitting my mom; although I found strange, disturbing stories. In North Carolina I read about the discovery of a young woman who took a nasty spill down a mountain. Her clothing torn to shreds and her face, hands and legs bruised and bleeding. She lay in a hospital bed in a catatonic state. The police believed she witnessed a brutal murder across the street from her home. Although intriguing the story had nothing to do with my search. I clicked off the page getting back on track. The coffee house was closing. In the morning I'd get up early and visit the public library.

At the library the next day, I again searched like a hound dog chasing a fox. My eyes went buggy from reading the computer screen, then something caught my eye. A young girl, fifteen, went missing at approximately the same year my mom would have turned fifteen. There was a picture, and the girl looked like a young version of my mom - freckles, long light hair, dark eyes, approximate weight 95 lbs., a height of five feet. Her name was Perdita Ferguson and her parents were Thane and Leila Ferguson. I pulled my tablet with questions out of my backpack, scribbled the information onto a blank paper inside and continued searching, looking for an address. I found one in Georgia. Her parent's strange names made address finding possible, had they been Jane or John Smith' I'd never found them.

After three days, James produced my new identity. LulaBell, now a stunning, shapely young woman, and James transported me to the local bus station. My ID said I was twenty-one-year-old Shanna Nu. As I stepped out of the car, I slipped him an envelope with a wad of cash. "It's time for me to leave again. Thank you so much for your help and making me of legal drinking age." I gave him a huge bear hug.

The corners of his mouth turned upwards at the ends in a smile. "No problem, you find those answers. If you need help again, you know where to find me."

LulaBell stepped out of the truck, wrapped her arms around me and whispered, "Be careful, Cleo."

I wasn't sure how much she understood about her father's illegal dealings, although she wasn't a young child anymore, I imagined she understood quite a bit. I entered the station catching the next bus to Allentown, Georgia.

LulaBell's words stuck with me during the ride. *Be careful Cleo.* If only she knew the half of it. I had money from my nest egg, and self-defense skills that already paid off in Paris. Armed for battle and ready to uncover the secrets to my existence I plotted my moves. How would I approach Mr. and Mrs. Ferguson? I couldn't walk up to the Fergusons' door and tell them about their missing child/child abductor/junkie/murdered daughter. This situation must be approached with care, maybe I'd stake-out their home for a couple days. That's it! I had a kid's play police badge from my dumpster diving days, but it looked real at a quick glance. I'd pretend to be a detective and with respect pick their brains. With that in mind, I got off at the next stop, bought a navy-blue women's suit, a white blouse, along with conservative heels and a flip pad and blue pen. I'd wrap my hair into a bun going heavy on the makeup to appear older.

Jaw Dropper

Upon arrival in Dublin, Georgia - Allentown sat outside the city limits - the sun set as dusk settled. I checked into a motel for the night, stiff from the bus ride I perused the small city. My stomach gurgled nasty words, so I stopped at a bar and grill for dinner. As I ate, I reflected on how good it felt to be back in the States. In Paris I forgot how much I loved the U.S. and how vast its borders are, causing the perception I was looking for a needle in a haystack.

A young man uninvited, sat in the booth across from me and introduced himself, "Hi, I'm Bub Richards." He extended his hand in greeting. I didn't extend mine back. It floored me how he plopped into the booth like I invited him. He had soft blue eyes, chestnut wavy hair and a baby face - not too shabby to look at, but he had an awful lot of gall.

"I'm leaving, nice to meet you, Bub." I said standing up to leave.

"You're a dazzling beautiful woman and I couldn't help myself. I'm sorry." A poor try to remediate his failed attempt.

"Like I said, I'm leaving." I slipped money to the server and walked out the door.

No sooner did I walk out the door than I heard footsteps behind me. Fear surfaced inside me as the terrors of my past came rushing back. I slipped around the corner and waited. Soon enough, a form drew closer as I watched its shadow through the streetlights glide across the pavement. I positioned myself and brought my leg out in front of me as the shadow person walked past my spot. This caused him to trip and fall flat on his face. Familiar tufts of chestnut hair crashed forward.

"Bub? Oh, I'm so sorry. I thought maybe... nevermind. Why are you following me?" I offered my hand to help him up from the pavement. His nose was bloody. My self-defense skills affected people that way, I reflected, remembering when I threw Halette over my shoulder in Paris, twice.

He took my hand and sheepishly said, "I just think you're beautiful and wanted to know you better." Ay yi yi, what was it with men?

"OK, your nose is bleeding. I'll buy you a drink." A small pang of guilt crept into my soul.

His face lit up and a huge smile creased his lips as blood trickled down his chin in a slow but steady stream. "That'd be nice."

I bought him a drink while the bartender readied a rag and ice for his nose. "It might be broken." Pangs of guilt shot through my soul.

The bartender, a young dark-haired woman with surreal emerald eyes, chuckled. "He'll be okay. At least once a week he incurs the wrath of one young lady or another."

"So, you're a lady chaser and I was on the menu for tonight?"

His face turned as red as a tomato. "Can't we enjoy this drink before you run off again?" He stared into my eyes with ferocity, it made me uncomfortable. Then he drew closer. "You look a lot like that model. The one who's dating the really rich French guy, umm Jennifer... no Juniper... I got it" As if he found the pot of gold at the end of the rainbow he shouted, "Justine!"

Was it ever going to end? Would I always be Justine to people? "Sure, yup, that's me." His eyes grew wide and his mouth dropped from its jaw, I thought I would have to catch it and glue it back on his face. "I'm joking, allow me to introduce myself, since I bloodied your nose, I suppose it's the least I can do. I'm Shanna."

He picked his jaw off the ground. "Nice to meet you, Shanna. You aren't from here, cause I know everyone and no one beautiful as you lives anywhere near here. So, you visiting?"

Gees, were his syrupy pick-up lines ever going to stop? "No, more like business." I used my best cop voice as practice before meeting the "grandparents" tomorrow and picked his brain since he claimed he *knew* everyone.

"Have you met Thane and Leila Ferguson?"

"Oh yeah, Thane was a mean S.O.B. when he drank liquor. Heart disease killed him, maybe it was something else, but he's dead. Leila is a sweet lady, real quiet, always home." A mean drunk father, no wonder my mom ran.

Bub and I enjoyed several drinks before he insisted on giving me his number and attempting to go back to my cheap motel room with me. I gave him a peck on the cheek and told him good night. He

would never be aware that he met the
famous Justine Holmes.

Perdita

I awoke early the following morning and headed to Allentown by way of taxi, which I thought blew my cop persona, but it couldn't be helped. I never learned to drive anything larger than a golf cart. Their house was small and their yard in desperate need of help. The overgrown grass and plants looked as though at one time the yard must have been picturesque; daisies, marigolds and tulips peeked between the weeds around the house. Morning glories coiled around the dilapidated fence swallowing it. Two plastic chairs and a table sat to the side under a makeshift covered porch in front of the house.

As I pressed the doorbell button it popped off the wall and hung by two colored cords. I tried knocking. When nobody answered, I walked around the house, and saw an elderly woman bent over, somewhat tending an overgrown garden. My assumption was, this is Mrs.

Ferguson, my grandmother - well aware Perdy kidnapped me. I walked up to her, and she stood. "Can I help you?" Her gray hair was thinning and wrinkles webbed across her face. She had a small frame and a slight hunch curved her back.

I answered while I flashed my badge quick as possible, so she wouldn't notice it was a fake. "I hope so, ma'am. Are you Mrs. Ferguson?"

She eyed the badge, but not too close. "I am, would you like to come in and have some lemonade? I've been in the garden all morning; it's time for a break."

I followed her up to the porch where she motioned me to sit down in one of the plastic chairs. The porch was in such poor condition, I feared it would crumble beneath my feet. She disappeared inside the small house. Then reappeared with a plastic pitcher and glasses on a weathered plastic serving tray - Georgia fine china.

I opened the door for her. As she poured the lemonade, I spoke in my most police-like voice. "Mrs. Ferguson, you had a daughter, Perdita, who disappeared about twenty-six years ago." I opened my flip pad and cleared my throat for extra cop-like effect. "May I ask you some questions?"

"Perdy, yes, that's been so long ago. So long ago..." She seemed nostalgic.

"Would you have any pictures of her I could look at?" My voice police-like but with a touch of true concern. I had to see color pictures to be positive.

"Yes, yes, please come in." She reminded me of a black and white TV show mom whom all the neighborhood kids loved and went to her house for milk and cookies.

The inside of her home was clean and organized, but the furniture must have been as old as Perdita. Leila rummaged around in a chest and brought out a single photo album. She showed me pictures of Perdy throughout her childhood. This child was without a doubt my mom - her eyes, hair, freckles, and facial expressions. Memories of Perdy flooded my mind and sorrow mixed with anger arose in my heart. I gulped back my emotions. "Mrs. Ferguson when Perdy disappeared was she having any trouble in school?"

"She was a good girl, but always had trouble with her grades. She didn't read or write well, but she had friends." Mrs. Ferguson was compliant, I didn't want to push my luck, but I wanted - needed to know more.

"How about at home?"

"She… never got along well with her father. He was a hard man. He's gone now. Cirrhosis of the liver."

"I'm sorry to hear that, Mrs. Ferguson." My heart bled for her, missing daughter, dead husband, and now alone. "Did anything happen between them the night before she disappeared?"

"Yes, yes… she hung out with a young man. Her father didn't approve of him. He thought he… Her father had opinions and said the young man would take advantage of her. You understand?"

"Yes, of course. We worry for our children." I didn't have any, but she didn't know that. "Could you describe the young man?"

"It was so long ago. Let me think… brown eyes, long brown hair that hung over his face, like a sheepdog. I don't reckon he brushed it much. His name was…" She remained quiet for a minute until his name clicked in her mind. "Frank Tomey, but he liked to be called Slug."

Slug was my predator, but Frank Tomey? I recognized the name and made a mental note to search my records when I got back to the motel. I slipped a picture of

Perdy out of its sleeve, and slid it into the bottom of my flip pad while Leila turned her head, then casually handed her back the single album.

She asked the question I dreaded. "Have you found my daughter?" Telling someone their child is dead is equal to stabbing them over and over with a pitchfork into the heart, although Mrs. Ferguson seemed to be accepting. I guess because so much time passed.

"Yes, we did, about seven years ago. We recently made the connection."

"Is she alive?" Her grave voice quivered.

I held back my own tears. "I'm sorry, but no. Her body was found... in a river... That is why I am here now. I wanted to make sure it was your daughter and give you a name you could contact to make arrangements for her, to bury her properly. Thank you for your time and I'm very sorry Mrs. Ferguson."

I scribbled Officer Han's name and number down and handed it to her, "Officer Han will assist you."

"Thank-you." Tears filled her eyes, but she seemed happy, peaceful, not remorseful. I understood and felt envy.

Now she had closure, something I wanted. I left.

My mother, or Perdy, didn't grow up in a big house, but she had a mom who loved and cared for her. On the flip side, her heavy-handed drunk father assisted in getting her mixed up with Slug. The story started making sense. How did I fit into the picture?

Back at the motel, I rummaged through my research. Frank Tomey, A.K.A. Slug killed Einstein. If Slug was still in jail, he wouldn't be a threat, but who was he? I read the article again. The pieces hadn't fit the first time. I read it again and they still didn't fit. Slug was a fall guy, but for whom?

I rolled the information over in my mind. My mom ran away at fifteen because of Slug, or to escape her abusive father. She and Slug were friends. Had she crossed him? I looked at the letters again. They met every three years at various places. The letter referred to me: *bring the girl*. She always came home with money. She blackmailed him! No, not him! He didn't have anything. Who did she blackmail? A deal gone wrong? He was a fall guy but for whom? She blackmailed his employer! How did I fit into this? She used me to blackmail his employer! That had to be it! Now I needed to find his employer.

I never checked to see if the Tomato Shack was a real place, so I withdrew my phone from its slot in my purse and did a map search. It was a real place of business, a restaurant. Tanwood Dr.; their other meeting place existed too. Both were in California, an hour's drive from the shack I lived in with Perdy playing my mom. I saved the address in my phone map, then emptied the contents of my backpack onto the floor and rummaged through my history, jotting the names I discovered so far onto my notepad. I used the motel's guest computers to do internet searches and found little - one name stood out, with a fantastic opportunity attached to it. My next stop the West Coast City by the Bay.

Officer La Tige

My first order of business was getting a job, and I had my sights set on just the one: *La Tige Investigative Services.* La Tige the ex-cop who worked Perdy's, my kidnapper/mother's, case while he was on the force when her battered and beaten body turned up in the river.

Etched into the frosted glass door read *Detective La Tige Private Investigative Services*. Inside, the office a small wooden desk covered in clutter sat in a corner. A large man with his back turned away from the door sat on the edge of a well-worn pleather chair talking on the phone. I waited. After several minutes he turned around and introduced himself.

"Jim La Tige, may I help you?" He leaned further into the chair, resting his back.

"Yes, I'm inquiring about the receptionist position?"

"Yes, yes, my last receptionist left four weeks ago and as you can see," he gestured to the scattered piles atop his desk, "I'm in need of another. Too many jobs going to keep the office neat. Any recent job experience?"

"No, but if you give me a chance, I'll organize this place and have it running smooth in no time." I never worked a real job, except modeling as Justine, but I needed a job and specifically *this* job, so I turned on my charm and puckered out my chest.

"No experience. Can you answer a phone?" His eyes did a quick glance across my chest, then back to my face. Well, at least he wasn't being picky, and from the condition of his office, he was in desperate need.

"Yes." I flashed him a sweet smile.

"Can you file alphabetically and numerically?"

What kind of idiot couldn't? I went to the row of filing cabinets, picked up a file marked with a blue colored dot then found the cabinet with blue dots and looked at the alphabetically filed drawers - A-G/ H-N/ O-Z. I opened the A-G drawer, flipped through until I got to the G's, next Garcia's, Gomez, Jose, Mary and Richard.

"Impressive! The job is yours. I need to make a copy of your driver's license and social security card. While I do that, fill out these papers." A hint of rush in his voice.

"I don't have a driver's license, but I have a passport. Will that do?"

"That'll work." I pulled it out of my purse. He took it in his hand and eyeballed it. "Twenty-two, how's it you have no license?"

"Public transportation has always done me well and cars pollute, adding to ozone depletion and global warming." A quick save which rolled off my tongue like melted butter.

"Humph... You'll fit right in here in Frisco, lots of tree huggers." A correct observation, although not in the way he assumed. San Francisco was a place of beauty and freaks - I blended. At night it sparkled with magic and glowed with excitement - everybody unique and every corner of the city its own world.

He pulled a chair up to his desk, grabbed his file piles placing them on the floor. Then he handed me a pen, a form, and shuffled his approximate six-foot bulk to the copy machine, which made loud swooshing, kerchunking noises. I never filled out a tax form. My name I got, but exemptions. I filled in 0's and signed. I handed it back to him, he shook my hand, gave me back my passport and social security card. He picked up the pile of files from the floor and shoved them into my hands.

"I'll return in an hour," he grumbled, and with that disappeared out the door, which I found odd since he just hired me.

Now I could access more information than on the internet alone. Officer La Tige's brain would be assistance to my investigation too. I wasn't using him. After all, he desperately needed someone to keep things organized and under control, and I needed to solve my own mystery, so I thought it a fair trade. I found what I was looking for and tumbled headfirst into it.

Officer La Tige, or P.I. La Tige. - nah, officer, sounded more official - was a large man of few words. He stood six feet tall with a bulky, muscular build, and a slight but noticeable limp in his left leg. Thick tufts of dark brown hair infused with gray spirals framed his head accentuating his square shaped face. His eyes were a stunning blue, which offset his rhinoceros-like appearance. He was straight and to the point, and didn't talk much about himself or anything else, rather he barked orders. He lacked social graces and was intimidating. I understood why he had a difficult time keeping a receptionist. The only way to get anything personal out of him would be to gain his trust. I came in every day and did my job -- nothing less, but always more.

Kacy's Cocktail

My next order of business was to find more permanent housing accommodations in the expensive city I lived. By accident I found a place. I looked at an overpriced studio, which I could afford - barely. The approximate 600 square feet apartment overlooked nothing but roadway located in what is called the *Mission District*.

The realtor Mrs. Fairway, with her buggy eyes protruding out of their sockets and a straight line for a smile, handed me the rental application, which I filled out on the spot. She then took it, and scrunched her straight, thin lips into a smile. "Thank you, Ms. Nu." She propped the application in front of her eyes and held it at a distance. "And we will get back to you within the next two weeks as the place has just come on the market." She opened the door gesturing for my exit. It had been the same everywhere I looked, and I had no experience in the department of finding an apartment. I hoped for a male realtor, but alas, no.

Lights blinked brightly in unison, reading *Happy Trails,* above the bus stop. Below, more lights flashed *Happy Hour $2.00 draft beer.* My mind, followed by my body, walked inside and plopped onto the only vacant stool. It was difficult trying to make a legitimate life without gorgeous, loving Didier to take care of me. I missed him, Sam, Jean - hell, the whole hotel crew. Just a few weeks ago I lived a dream life that many people would kill for, now I was a world away, and Paris felt like a distant memory. In the bar people came, people went, guys attempted to hit on me, walking away empty handed. Six drafts later, I sat in the same stool.

A female voice spoke. "Holding up the bar. Is it that bad?"

"For tonight." I mumbled back, my shoulders slumped and elbows resting on the bar. I didn't even look up at her.

The voice chuckled. "What's so bad you turned away my hottest male customers?"

I looked at her for the first time. Her dark eyes appeared as velvet stepping stones leading to her soul. "Apartment hunting."

"Oh well, in that case…" She turned from me, dumped shots from a few bottles of liquor into a shaker and poured the concoction into two small gold rimmed glasses. She then pushed the liquors and shaker towards me and glided around the bar. She did everything with such ease she appeared to float. "To us," she said, raising her glass. We both sucked back the sweet drink as if it were nectar.

"That's really good. What is it?"

"I call it Kacy's cocktail. I'm Kacy and this is my bar." She splayed her hands out in opposite directions. The bar consisted of little more than a long wooden bar with a fully stocked liquor cabinet and a few wooden tables. We continued to drink Kacy's cocktails, with older rock music playing in the background, and talked until closing. She inherited the bar when her father passed away a few months back. At first, she considered selling it and finishing her degree, but changed her mind as it had been a solid piece of her childhood in the city she loved.

"College wasn't working too well anyway. I was pursuing a degree in education, and when I learned how they are taking away teacher privileges, such as tenure, and wanting to pay them based on bullshit instead of hard work. I rethought my major. Then dad passed and here I am, the happy owner of all this." A smile creased her oval face as her velvet eyes scanned all 500 square feet of the bar.

A young Hispanic man with a solid, handsome face and eyes as velvety as hers walked in, wrapped his arms around her, and planted a long, sensuous kiss upon her lips. I thought of Didier and the many occasions we embraced in such a similar way. "This is Shanna, and she is looking for an apartment." Her velvets reached into my soul. "Shanna this is Javier, my boyfriend."

He extended me his hand. "It's nice to meet you, Shanna."

I met his hand with mine. "It's a pleasure to meet you." He was a knockout with thick chocolate hair, deep brown-black eyes and a tush any man-wanting woman would love to grab.

Kacy turned her attention back to me, and her face lit up like an Alabama yard decorated for Christmas. "I have a two-bedroom apartment above the bar, and I would really like a roommate, but the bar keeps me so busy I haven't placed an ad yet. Come, take a look."

We stumbled outside, bumping into walls while staggering up a staircase, holding one another for drunken support. I couldn't believe my dumb luck. The apartment wasn't big, although its size made me realize the bar was much larger than I previously thought as it covered the entire length of it. She offered me an unbelievable rate, which I accepted. I slept on her sofa that night and the following morning she and Javier drove me to the low budget inn I had been staying at while I grabbed my sparse belongings and checked out.

It turned out Javier was a grad student at U.C. Berkeley and only stayed with her on the weekends. They were both natives of the area. Kacy and I formed a fast friendship. I admired her strength, youthfulness and vitality, which were lackluster at best inside me.

"Nu"

Within a few days I organized La Tige's office. I learned the colored dots on the files and drawers stood for the type of case: blue meant a cheating spouse; green meant a missing person; red meant a missing item; yellow stood for miscellaneous; and white meant unsolved. He had the file cabinets arranged alphabetically and the information in the files arranged numerically by date. I worked out a more efficient system for billing clients, collecting money, paying bills, ordering office supplies, and all order of office management. He didn't like making out my paycheck every week, and so after a month I did that too.

He threw his cases, open and closed, onto my desk, making a slobbish mess of them. I did *not* appreciate it. "Do you have to throw them? You nearly knocked over my coffee! Your desk may look like a tornado rolled over it, but I like mine neat."

"So, I see." His eyes scanned the length of my desk. "Lunch?"

"Yes. Thanks." I accepted and sensed we were bonding. He took me to a Mexican joint where we stuffed our faces with mega-sized burritos washed down with beer. Where else can a person drink on the job, paid for by the boss? As he ate, food stuck to his five o'clock shadow and dropped onto his tray. He was as messy at eating as he was with everything else.

"You are a man of many words."

He humphed with a mouth full of food, pieces falling to his tray.

"We walked past an office supply store on the way here. We're stopping there on the way back. There are a few things we need." I could make demands too.

He swallowed his food this time and spoke instead of humphing. "Yeah, OK." Then he wiped his face, displaying he had at least some social graces.

At the store we purchased two wire, metal bins. I labeled them "closed" and "open" and placed them on the file cabinets beside my desk.

He was a surly man who barked orders, although I could be every bit as tough. He met his match, which I believe he respected. I still had a job anyway. We reached a pinnacle in our relationship that afternoon. He went from throwing things and growling orders at me to calling me Nu, 'Hey Nu... Nu I need...' in one day.

In the following weeks his respect grew turning into trust. Maybe out of necessity or laziness, but his trust seemed genuine. He didn't like doing research and left that for me. My mind mulled over whether he ever entrusted his past secretaries to the level he did me. Various data banks on the computer pulled up different types of information on people such as criminal records, addresses, phone numbers, and more. He provided me with the passwords, handed me a key to the office, and gave me a cell phone; a huge gesture.

"Nu, you'll need these. The passwords, memorize and shred. The key, put on your key ring. The phone, only use to contact me. I'm leaving town for a few days for a case." The affectionate term 'Nu', brought me up several notches from receptionist to respected, trusted co-worker. He then added, "Don't call me on it. I prefer texts."

I hadn't begun my own research yet because I first wanted to gain his trust, have an ally. La Tige crept into the ranks of cohort. I wanted to pick his brain about my mom's case - there were details in it I could use to find relevant familial information. I was in no immediate hurry and La Tige was opening doors for me. After a few months of running and managing his office, he took me out after work to an undisclosed location. He stopped at a shooting range and pulled out a gun.

"You ever use one of these?"

"Yes, my dad used to take me to the range when I was a kid." A big, fat lie, but harmless. Lies controlled my life since conception.

"Very good."

A drab, dismal gray building inside and out housed the shooting range. We checked in and put on large headphone things. La Tige called them ear muffs. His blue eyes looked square into my eyes as he pulled the pistol from his belt.

"Show me what you got." He offered me the gun, which I accepted, lowering it away from people as Sam taught me. I clicked off the safety, then brought the gun to my sights, and fired. The bullet whizzed and landed just above the center of the target. "Not bad." He tilted his box-head to the side and grinned. It was the first sign of a smile I had seen on his face.

"Guess I'm a bit rusty." It pleased me the bullet landed near the target.

"I need you to hit the target this time." For the next trial I put a bullet into the center of the target's head.

"That's impressive!" He exclaimed. Emotion, he showed emotion. Now that impressed me.

Overall, he seemed fascinated and taught me new tricks about holding a gun and how to shoot. I assumed he brought me to the range as a friendly social gesture to end a long week. I felt a tinge of a bond forming. Something more than work-friendship. I hadn't been close to many people and possibly was making more of his gesture than was present.

He placed his gun back into its holster positioned around his waist. "Thirsty?"

"Yeah, and I know a great little bar," I offered thinking of Happy Trails and Kacy.

"Let's roll." Into his older model Monte Carlo beast-vehicle which screamed 'bath me' we climbed. Burrito, taco wrappers, and empty cardboard coffee mugs littered the inside of his car - the odor reminiscent of a sweaty armpit.

La Tige's car sputtered to a halt behind Happy Trails. As we walked through the door Kacy greeted us. "Hey Shanna and Mr. Straight Face."

"It's La Tige."

"Well, La Tige, welcome to Happy Trails. What can I get you?"

The corners of his mouth turned up into a smile. "Two beers on my tab and keep 'em coming."

"You big spender." Kacy wrinkled her nose and dashed her dark velvets at him.

We took a table and took part in real conversation. It wasn't my imagination; we were connecting. "I used to come here in my cop days. A man ran it then." I could feel the doors of trust opening with that tidbit of information from his cop days.

"How long were you a cop?" I wanted to keep the doors open, partly for knowledge about my mom's sordid past, and partly because I started thinking of him as something more than my boss.

"Shot In the leg. They put me behind a desk and I filed for early retirement. Soon after, I opened my P.I. business. I need action, not paperwork." Sorrow evident in his voice.

"Yeah, I've gotten that impression." I chuckled. "What made you become a cop?"

"My father, grandfather, hell, all of 'em were cops, and good ones." He was opening up, so I eased into asking about his cases, such as the most intriguing, most frustrating and last, the unsolved. I wanted to tread light, to avoid halting the conversation.

When we got to unsolved cases, he brought up my mom's case. "Several years ago, just before I retired, we had a case. A young woman, beat up bad from the river and her attacker, turned up floating in the Bay just beyond the mouth of the Sacramento River. No records on her - like she never existed. We never ID'd her. No one claimed the body, so she went into a Jane Doe grave - case closed."

"That's sad, no family, no friends. How does someone die without being missed?" I asked with too much contemplation in my voice. He shot his blue eyes at me, which delved straight into my heart, almost as if he was reaching for confirmation from me.

"My ex-partner called me not long ago. Said a cop visited her elderly mother and gave her his number. Not on a card as is customary, but wrote it down for her. This woman's daughter went missing at fifteen.

The authorities exhumed the body, everything matched, and her mother gave her a proper burial. Still don't know who murdered her, but she got a real funeral. Everybody deserves at least that."

I fought to control the sadness and tears threatening to burst from my eyes. Leila buried my kidnapper mother. An emptiness filled my soul.

His steely blues still searched my soul, waiting for something from me. He had been forthcoming, but I wasn't ready yet. I guess trust is a two-way street. After what seemed like a long silence, but in reality, mere seconds, I answered, "She got a real funeral and her mother got closure. Maybe that's enough." Our roles reversed, now I was the one lacking conversational skill.

"Han, my ex-partner, said that officer was her guardian angel. Strangest part of all of it - no officer from any precinct within either area reported as going to see her." Without question that was the largest amount of words he spoke to me at any single time.

We sat quiet for a moment, each deep in thought... "Something else strange: my partner got an anonymous tip a few years back. Nothing more panned out though;

just a couple pairs of fingerprints. One matched the victim, the other unknown." He reached, probed inside my soul for something, but how could he know? Cop's hunch? I gave him nothing more. I was content in knowing that my kidnapper foster mother, Perdy, had at least a funeral with her own mother present.

It's Time You Learn

The following day La Tige entered the office, tossing his keys at me. "Let's roll."

I grabbed the keys before they hit my chest. "You're gonna need these." I offered handing the jingling set back to him.

"Nope, you're driving. About time you learn, Nu." He stated with no qualms.

"Oh, no, no, no. I've never driven anything larger than a golf cart."

"Golf cart? Aren't you refined?"

"A challenge? OK, let's roll." I didn't want to learn to drive in his beast of a vehicle, but I refused to take his not so subtle ridicule either.

The beast vehicle's front seat swallowed me whole, my feet resting nowhere near the pedals. At least I didn't have to toss empty cardboard coffee mugs to the back seat to sit. La Tige was no help in showing me the buttons and knobs I needed to adjust my seat and mirrors. Instead, he sat quiet stifling a laugh. As I rooted around for the controls, I found quite a few; unfortunately, not the ones I needed, causing the seat to bounce up and down like a low-rider with hydraulics and the wipers to swoosh across a dry windshield. By the time I situated myself and my feet were close enough to touch the brake and gas pedals he was laughing so hard tears streaked his square face.

"You could have helped." I made no attempt to hide my sarcasm.

"Oh no, watching you was priceless. You did good."

He soon became more cooperative and directed me to the ignition, although not before he showed me what the gauges and protruding chrome knobs on the dash did. This was going to more difficult than driving a golf cart. The engine started up with a roar and leaped forward with force when I pressed the accelerator.

"Easy, go light on the gas. This baby's got eight cylinders and plenty of horses under the hood." Why would someone put horses under the hood? A question better left unanswered.

My uneasiness behind the wheel intensified as he made me drive all over San Francisco, up and down hills and around curves. I either took the turns too sharp or too loose. At the top of each hill loomed a stop sign - nothing below visible, like stop signs to the edge of nothingness. I underestimated the stopping power of the beast on flat roads and more haphazard on hilly roads, nearly catapulting us into the windshield my first few stops. We were fortunate the old car had functioning seatbelts.

"Do you think about how much pollution this beast of yours puts into the air?"

"Never. Keep driving." As he spoke the words, his phone rang to the tune of "Bad to the Bone". "La Tige... yup." Hanging up the call he turned towards me, "Nu, follow that sign. Got somewhere to be." That sign was the on ramp to the Bay Bridge.

"A bridge. A big bridge with lots of traffic. You can't be serious. I've almost killed us at least twice driving up and down these crazy hilly roads!" I yelped with true fear in my quivering voice.

"Dead serious. You'll be fine. Wouldn't ride with you if I thought you'd kill me."

'You'll be fine'. I didn't have confidence in that statement. I reminded myself to breathe as we plowed forward onto the bridge. We rode in the edge lane which I hated, the water beneath us visible, but fear secured me to it. I forced myself to remember the other near-death experiences in my life as we cruised across the bridge.

"You don't have to drive like a granny here. Open her up."

Open what up? I questioned within the confines of my mind, although I knew perfectly well what he meant. It was fear that froze my ability to place more force on the accelerator. "I don't think so." The side of the bridge closed in on us. The water below flowed in wild torrents while the wind rushed hard against the vehicle.

"Relax," was all I heard before the blackness took me.

The Other Side

"Nu, Nu." Stated a familiar male voice as I gained consciousness. The first few minutes my mind was groggy. When it cleared, I recognized we were in a vacant parking lot.

"What? How? We were on the bridge. Everything went black." Incoherent sentences ran like diarrhea from my mouth.

"You passed out a few paces from the exit. I coasted the car into this parking lot." Voiced a calm, cool La Tige.

"What, how?" I'm not sure why it surprised me La Tige seemed capable of the impossible.

"Doesn't matter. You're awake. We gotta roll again."

Relief washed over me as I realized I no longer sat in the driver's seat and the menacing bridge was behind us.

Within fifteen minutes we coasted into another parking lot housing a set of dingy gray office buildings. He shifted into park and the beast sputtered as he cut off the engine.

"Stay here."

Every bit of Oakland I'd seen looked the same - gray and depressing. I wondered if a brighter, happier part of this dismal city existed.

Thirty minutes or more passed before I saw La Tige's bulky, limping form exit the building. In that time, I crouched low in the car with the doors locked. The foreboding appearance of the city placed my mind back to my younger street years and sent a chilling reminder of Einstein's death. I clicked the button unlocking the doors as La Tige reached out to grab the door handle.

He got into the beast-vehicle and roared up the engine without saying a word. Not that he ever said much. We drove through Oakland and back over the bridge, now not so menacing since I was in the passenger seat, before I broke the ice.

"So, what was that about?"

"A client." Typical La Tige, short, sweet, and to the point.

"Can you give me a few details?" I questioned as the cloak and dagger thing just didn't cut it for me.

"Thinks his wife is cheating. You hungry?"

"I could eat." As the statement left my vocal cords, I realized how La Tige sounding it was.

The Tomato Shack

I worked up the courage over a weekend to visit the places my mom frequented, according to the letters, every three years with Slug. The Tomato Shack was a divey little sub sandwich shop outside Sacramento. The blue paint on the outside peeled and cracked from sun and lack of upkeep. Each window displayed the ad, *Lunch Sandwich Special 12 inch Sub Plus Large Drink and Bag of Chips $5.00*, along with multiple sets of fingerprints. Inside, dirt built up in the corners of the tile floor, and dark mucky splotches muddled the walls. The whole place reminded of an unclean public restroom. The counter and tables looked clean, although I doubted bleach had touched them for years.

A young girl, no more than sixteen, stood behind the counter. She twisted at her blond ringlets while smacking on what sounded like an entire package of bubble gum, her hands gliding over the screen of her phone. I grasped she wouldn't be able to provide me any info, although I figured it wouldn't hurt to ask. She glanced my way with steely, battleship-gray eyes as I approached the counter, "Ready to order?" she asked, placing her phone on the counter with a sigh like I was intruding on her.

I flipped my P.I. card at her. "I'm looking for information. Is there a manager or owner whom I could speak with?"

"My dad owns the place. He'll be in tomorrow." Her words came out in spurts between chomps, followed up with a mega-sized bubble I expected to pop all over her face. She sucked it back in without a single strand sticking to her face. Her blank stare told me her synapses halted firing and her brain was a few walnuts shy of the tree.

"Thanks, about what time?"

Chomp, chomp, smack. Her eyes jolted to life alerting me that her synapses were back online. "'Bout one in the afternoon."

"I'll be back then."

My next stop was 1523 Tanwood Dr. Rows of duplexes lined the street on both sides circling around a cul-de-sac. The construction was '80s style with lackluster brown paint on each and every cloned home. 1523 sat on the outer edge of the cul-de-sac. I walked up the street, contemplating what to say. I considered this place had been something to Slug, not my mother, and many years passed since he'd sent the letter. Neighborhoods like these were transient, revolving doors for people trying to make a start or dealing drugs. Thoughts flopped around in my head something like a lizard's tail missing its body. The front door coming ever closer with each step.

The door now stared me in the face, the doorbell a hands length away. Without warning heavy metal music blasted like an automatic rifle against my eardrums, and the sound of a sputtering engine halted me in my tracks. I turned to see a late model Camaro pulling into the driveway. A fortyish man stepped out of the vehicle, a mane of thick brown hair flowed in a bad mullet from his head, a denim jacket minus sleeves covered his torso. The sleeves handmade judging by the frazzled ends of the fabric around his arms, with a black rock T underneath, and jeans that boasted more holes than my worst pair during my homeless days, covered his legs. "I'm not buying, so go away," sputtered off his lips with a vengeance.

Did I look like a saleswoman in my jeans and T-shirt? His obvious negativity towards me resonated inside my head, forcing me to make up a story and quick. "No, no, I'm not here selling anything. In fact, I'm hoping you can help me?"

"You're a little young for me, but maybe we can work something out." He murmured edging ever closer attempting to invade my space. I felt uncomfortable, and thoughts of planting my foot straight into his most prized bodily possession lingered at the edge of reality. Carefully, I chose my words, "Are you Frank Tomey?"

I knew Slug, Frank, or whoever, was sitting inside a jail cell; however, I meant business. He stopped a few feet from me; narrowed his eyes into tiny slits while rolling his fat sickly yellowish tongue across his lips. "Frank. What do you want with him?" Satisfaction overwhelmed me. He knew him. My fabrication formulated with every word that sprung from my mouth.

"I believe I'm his daughter. Many years ago, he dated my mom." At this point I pulled out the picture of Perdy I lifted from her mother's and poised it in front of his face.

"I never seen her and haven't talked to Frank in a decade." His eyes prickled at me to go away, and with each ensuing second that passed the air thickened with tension. I stood my ground, an out of shape, '80s castaway was no match for me.

I drilled him with my cold hard stare until he relented. "Alright, Frank is my kid brother but we don't talk. He got messed up in some bad shit I didn't need rolling back on me."

I continued my glare, attempting to boil information from his innards. "I didn't know he had a kid; doubt he knew he had a kid. You gonna keep staring me down?" Since studying La Tige's tactics this had been my first opportunity to use them and they worked far better than I expected. Sweat drops bubbled on his forehead. "He's in jail, killed some kid a few years ago. He's not a good guy. Not even when he was a young pup. Always played dirty."

Now that he was talking, I dared to reenter the conversation using the sympathy card. "I'm not looking for him to be a father figure. I just want to know about him."

"It's been a long night. Can this wait?"

"No, it took me days, and switching several busses to get here after finding a love letter he wrote to my mother asking her to meet him here, and to bring me." I fudged the love letter thing, thinking that my continued appeal to his compassionate side would at least get me in the door.

He rolled his eyes. "A love letter? He's a psychopath, an extreme narcissist." He flopped his hands to his sides in surrender. "Come in. I'll tell you what I got." And whatever I asked he answered.

The tales he told were too far-fetched not to be true. "Frank left home at 17, went to Georgia, or Alabama. I forget. He hooked up with some chick, I'm guessing your mom. Then he got a big job in New York working as an enforcer for a rich, powerful family named Britt or Bridge, Bridd? I figured they were mafia, but the name sounded English. I'd figured it would be Scarletti or something Italian. After that he'd come visit every few years. Driving a truck, I'm on the road a lot, so I'd let him crash here. He talked big about his job, being the muscle for that family puffed up his self-centered ego. After a while I didn't hear from him no more. He's my brother, but he's a bad egg, so I didn't miss him. Then several years ago, he calls me from jail. Hadn't heard from him in years and suddenly he wants money for a lawyer." He clicked his tongue. "He's not head smart, but I can't remember him ever mentioning a kid."

I pondered his words, swishing them around mentally. "I don't think he wanted much to do with me. She raised me alone, never said a word about who my father was. When I grew old enough to ask, she blew it off, changing the subject. I found the letters while snooping around her room." It wasn't a total embellishment; at least the snooping and single mom things were true. He gave me Slug's (Frank's) address in prison. One day I'd pay old Slug a visit, but not until I fit the puzzle pieces together.

The following day arrived with a chill in the air and fog so dense I couldn't see my hand in front of my face. By noon a carpet of blue sprawled across the sky, and the fog dissipated without leaving a trace. The sandwich shop looked just as dismal and murky as the previous day. A pimply faced young man replaced gum-smacking blondie at the counter. I went through the same routine without squandering a single second. "I was here yesterday and a young blond girl told me the owner would be in today?"

"Dad, a lady's here to see you!" He hollered. His buzz cut moved as his mouth opened.

A family-run business, perhaps he didn't sell enough sandwiches to hire real help. Within a few minutes a staunch, grossly overweight man shuffled towards me. His eyes were tiny beads set inside rolls of dough, and large wet stains filled the cloth beneath his armpits, I noticed as he offered me his hand, mumbling something that sounded like, "What can I help you with?"

I shook his pudgy, cold, clammy hand. "I work for a P.I. We're looking for a woman. She used to frequent here about fifteen years ago." I pulled out Perdy's picture, which he took and examined, holding it an arm's length from his face.

He rubbed his available hand across his mouth and nose as if deep in thought, his chest heaved in and out. "I remember her. She met a man in the parking lot once, called the police on him. He hit her right outside the door, and knocked her on the ground; her nose was flowing like a sieve. Scared my customers."

I looked around at the vacant shop attempting to envision people eating here. He must have read my body language. "This place used to get business, high school kids, daytime regulars, until crime moved in and everyone else moved out. Police cleaned it up, but it's too late, everyone's gone." His voice laced with melancholy for the booming place his restaurant had been.

He talked in short sentences, followed by heavy breathing as if each word formed was a struggle. I felt no need to keep this man talking or reflecting on a time past. I had enough. I'd call the sheriff's office tomorrow and get the police report faxed.

Fetch

After spending a few hours jumping busses from Sacramento to San Francisco the warm glow and rhythmic beat of Happy Trails coaxed me into spending the rest of my evening at the bar. A few customers dotted the wood slab, and Kacy's eyes lit up when she saw me.

"My prodigal roommate." Kacy teased as I took a vacant seat at the bar.

"Spent the weekend in Sacramento, work related." Another lie, I longed to tell her the truth.

"Sacramento, girl you need one of these." She said while pouring various liquors into a shaker, transferring them to a glass, and handed me the blended result.

"Thanks!" The concoction tasted like candy.

I couldn't say what caused my next reaction. Before I knew it, I flew off my stool, and swayed my hips, across the vacant space in front of the bar. My body gyrated to the beat, up and down, and twirling from one step to the next. My hands combed my hair. I closed my eyes and let the music consume me until I was the music flowing through the small room.

Warm, small female hands grabbed onto mine. I opened my eyes and Kacy bumped to the beat in front of me, holding my hands. "My Dancing Queen. Abba ain't got nothing on you."

"Abba?" I questioned matching her moves beat for beat.

"Girl, the song. Sometimes I think you grew up under a rock." Kacy chuckled, her velvets sparkling like silk under the lights.

"I did." And that was the truth, well kinda.

She lifted my hand with hers, allowing me to twirl beneath her arms. We mimicked each other; our bodies moved together as a continuum. Slowly each man got off his well-worn bar stool and joined us - bumping, staggering, and swinging our hips. Liquid motion and laughter filled Happy Trails.

Tall, Dark, and Ever so Beautiful, danced closer and closer until his sterling silver eyes caught me in an intense visual moment. I swirled my body in the opposite direction, my eyes trailing off him with the movement, I danced with Short, Dumpy and Pear-shaped instead.

At this moment it struck me that I wasn't the frumpy gal I wanted Shanna to be nor Justine. I was me, Cleo. For the first time in my life I was free to live as I wanted, come and go as I pleased. No bodyguard or overprotective boyfriend. The need for survival no longer dictated my actions. I grew up, and the woman I turned into would always be Cleo, no matter what the guise. A sense of awareness drowned my soul. I couldn't hide under false names and identities forever. The woman inside me wouldn't allow it. To be free of my binding chains I needed to get to the bottom of my identity issues.

"You got moves." Said a male voice behind me. His body heat radiated against my back. I contorted my body sideways to observe my admirer, his chest centimeters from my face. Tall, Dark, and Ever so Beautiful. In that second the world froze as my eyes traced the outline of his broad shoulders, cruised up his neck, over his Adam 's apple, lingered on the five o'clock stubble that danced across his chin then rested on his silver bullet eyes. Our bodies coalesced into a single form undulating in waves of human lust. As the song wound down, he grabbed onto my hips, gyrating in sync towards the bar, a consuming, feverish wave drifted with us.

"Do you have a name?" The words played off his tongue.

"Shanna."

"Shanna, pleasure to meet you." He grasped my hand in his and placed a gentle kiss upon it.

The last thing I needed was another man in my life. I finally realized my fate and freedom was my own.

"Thanks for the dance." The edge in my voice evident as I stood and exited the bar.

An hour later Kacy trudged into the apartment. "That was awesome! I had no idea you could dance like that. What happened between you and Fetch?"

"Fetch?" I had to ask. I mean, who names their kid Fetch? Was he a pet in a previous life?

"Fletcher, but we call him Fetch."

"Nothing, not interested."

"Not interested? He's more beautiful than a god."

"He is. I'm not interested. I like my life the way it is."

Her velvet browns bore a hole into mine. "Babe, it's not like you're marrying him. Try some conversation, maybe a date?"

I remembered how quick I got caught up with Didier, who was every bit as tantalizing as Fetch. "Me and beautiful men have a track record that usually ends badly. My life is good. I don't need another gorgeous man making plans for my life."

She snuggled into the sofa, grabbing one of the puffy pillows which she brought to her chest. "Do tell."

I didn't want to lie to her. Everyday living with Kacy was like my girl day in Aruba. I decided on a diversion tactic. "Later, I have to get up and work in a few hours, good night."

"You're gonna spill eventually." Her words carried through the little apartment.

She was right. *Eventually* I would tell, but not yet.

Getaway Driver

"Hello." I slurred into the phone in a groggy state at five a.m. There was only one person it could be, La Tige; however, I wished he would tell me these things the day before instead of the pre-dawn morning of the event.

"Giving you the day off. Meet me seven tonight at the office. Got a stakeout, may need you." Then a click sounded on the other line as it went dead.

I managed a few more hours of sleep before slipping into the kitchen for rich delicious brew. I took my time sipping on my coffee, then headed downstairs to engage in actual human conversation.

"Morning sleepy-head. You look worse than me in the morning," joshed Kacy.

I slumped into a bar stool. "Early morning call from La Tige. Why doesn't he inform me the day before?"

"Honey, he's a tough man. He's got a soft spot for you though. I hear it in his voice and see it in his face. He's not the gushy type, but the 'I'm a man' type." She said deepening her voice, puffing up her chest while pushing out her elbows; her best La Tige impersonation.

"I guess."

The door swung open even though business hours hadn't yet approached. "Morning Shanna, Kacy."

"Uhhh…" I sighed pouring my arms over the bar and resting my face on the cold, slick wood as I recognized the sexy voice and remembered the mouth-watering body it belonged.

"Morning, Fetch." Kacy was far too perky.

"Ladies, two tickets to Candlestick were cast into my possession this morning for Sunday's game. I thought maybe Kacy, or Shanna," I felt his eyes resting on the top of my orange moppy hair sprawled across the bar, "would like to take advantage of this opportunity with me." His eyes hadn't moved, they penetrated inside my skull.

"Got a bar to tend and a boyfriend, remember?" The tone in her voice told me she was making an excuse, forcing me into hanging out with this gorgeous man for an afternoon.

"Shanna?" The sound waves from his voice hovered just above me.

I raised my head off the bar. "I'm busy too."

"No, you're not. I'll pick you up around…" He glanced at the spot on his wrist where a watch might sit, his was vacant, "eleven o'clock. That should give us tailgating time." With that he exited the bar, leaving me in a quandary.

"Did he really just do that?"

"He did." Kacy responded with a giggle. Her eyes lit up like New Years at Times Square. "He fancies you." She stated in a fake Fetch voice, raising her left eyebrow higher than her right.

"Uggh…"

At seven o'clock, as ordered by La Tige, I walked down the street to the office. "In the car!" He shouted from across the street. I veered into the road and took my seat next to him in the beast-vehicle. At least he was driving I reflected tossing a handful of burrito wrappers over my shoulder into the back seat. We headed out, taking the same trail to the gray set of office buildings we visited the day he forced me to drive.

"Our client, Mr. Nomes, believes his wife is cheating with his partner." He threw an envelope my way. In it were pictures of the wife and the partner, I assumed. The wife had red hair that flowed in waves around her face, sapphire blue eyes, and a body containing curves in all the right places and sizes. She couldn't have been much older than me. My first thought was 'that's what you get for having a trophy wife'. The man was at least twenty years her senior, with a full head of salt and pepper hair that lay flat against his skull, his eyes gray and steely. Fetch's silver eyes flashed through my mind, not gray, but silver, unusual.

"This is the man and woman we're looking for?"

"Sure is. According to Mr. Nomes, his partner, that guy." He pointed to the picture of the man. "Works late into the evening. He thinks they meet up at night. We'll follow him when he leaves and see where he goes. Get the camera out, and ready." La Tige barked.

I readied the camera.

An hour and twenty minutes later a tall, slim man silhouetted by the light left the building. The night was too dark, and few lights dotted the area, so I picked up the camera, zoomed in the lens and took a peak. "That's him."

He fired up the engine, left the lights off, and we waited until the man's vehicle left the parking lot. La Tige kept a careful distance between the man's car and ours. I snapped a picture of his license plate, and a couple when he left the dismal gray building. We trailed him to an old warehouse, instead of a luxury hotel. The man exited his vehicle, looked around, as if hiding something, then stole inside the building. I continued to snap pictures.

"Well, this is romantic." I said, hesitation in my voice.

La Tige shut off the engine and cocked his head to face me. "Yeah, something else is going on." He paused, then continued, "Stay here. I'm gonna get a closer view."

I watched his limping form until he disappeared. Every few minutes I used the camera's lens to survey my surroundings. This dismal city reminded me so much of my preteen years, running from one place to the next - rummaging through dumpsters, and the night I met Einstein, PeeWee, and Star, my friends and family for a short time. The memories flooded into my head.

The ringing of my phone startled me into the present. La Tige sent a text: *meet me round the front of building.* Was he crazy! The keys dangled in the ignition. My gaze shifted back and forth from the keys to the building, blowing out a deep 'ohh…' I slid across the long bench seat and started the car. Why, why, why? But I had to do it. La Tige was not only my boss, but I had grown fond of him, so I would drive. The beast roared into action. I shifted into drive, pressed lightly on the gas, and the car rolled out of its spot and through the parking lot. In an attempt to be covert, I chose not to turn the lights on. I nearly took out a trashcan rounding the corner. It swayed and rattled as the beast brushed by it with inches to spare.

La Tige's bulky form came into view. He ran-walk-limped to the car, practically diving into the passenger side. "Go and get the lights on!"

I switched the lights on and punched harder on the accelerator. The beast-vehicle accepted my request, and off we zoomed.

"Where are we going?"

"Turn left here. Catch up to the green sedan." He read off the plates using police or military code: Charley, Echo...

"I see him, there at the light. Stay over, don't get close."

I allowed his words to guide me as we cruised through Oakland, the Bay Bridge once again looming in the distance, getting closer each second. Oh Jeez, not again. Why couldn't he have his little affair with hussy on the Oakland side of the bridge?

"You can do this. Watch the road, keep an eye on your mirrors..."

He walked me through each step until we made it to the other side. "I did it. We're across!" One of my most monumental experiences to date.

"You did good. You still see him?"

"Two lights up. He's slowing."

The green sedan turned into a hotel parking garage. I cruised the car close to the curb, shifted into park, grabbed the camera, and turned to La Tige, "I got this." Not giving him a chance to respond, I jumped out of the car, slipped across the road, and snuck into the parking garage.

I slunk across the wall, my eyes searching for the green sedan. As soon as I spotted it, I found a dark corner and used the camera to locate him locked in an embrace with a brunette. I snapped pictures in consecutive motion as an actual photographer or paparazzo. The couple walked towards the elevator, opposite my location. With their backs towards me, I couldn't be sure it wasn't her, the wife. The brunette hair might be a wig.

I used spilt-second thinking and pulled the cord dangling from the camera around my neck to appear touristy, and stepped out of my corner, joining them at the elevator.

"Bee-utiful night, idn't it? This is m' ferst trip to San Fran-cisco and I jus cain't get over how bee-utiful it is." The couple seemed alarmed by my sudden appearance. "I'm so sorry, I forget to introduce m'self. Cleo, shat for Cleopaitra, cause m' daddy always said I look like an Egyptian princess. And ya are?"

"Not as happy to meet you," he said.

"Babe, that's rude." The mystery woman whispered towards him, a stern look on her face. It wasn't the wife. This woman was buxom as the wife, walnut brown hair framing her heart shaped face adorned by a set of amethyst colored eyes. She too was young. "I'm sorry, pleased to meet you Cleo. I'm Jeanne and this is my husband Fred. So, tell, where are you from?" She used an extra sugary voice.

"Georgia. Nice to meet ya." The elevator wound to a stop, and the doors glided open welcoming us. From the corner of my eye I spied him press the button for the third floor.

"Floor?"

"Three."

"Oh, goody," he said in a mocking tone.

I knew he was more than annoyed with my disruption to his evening with the lady, I looked him square in the eye and formed a large smile. She wasn't the woman and I should have gone back to the car; however, I didn't. My curiosity drove me.

The couple ran walked out of the elevator, giggling and whispering as they went. No doubt they were having fun at my expense. I walked behind them, fumbling in my pocket pretending to search for my key, as I walked up to room number 316. They never looked back at me and soon entered their room. The façade was over, and I wasn't sure what to do next, but someone else had other plans.

Abruptly, I turned on my heel to face a redhead, the redhead, Mrs. Nomes. Her flaming red big-hair gave her a gnome-like appearance. Inwardly, I laughed at my own observation. "I've been watching you sweety. What are you up to?" Oops, maybe he got bored and traded her in for a younger model, seeing her close up, she had to be at least thirty.

"I's just headin' back to ma car, lef ma room key thare." She scrunched her eyes and blinked several times. I may have gone too heavy on the accent. "Scuse me." I pushed past her, and felt her fingers grasp the camera cord around my neck, halting my forward motion and giving me a jerk.

"You're coming with me." Déjà vu, why did I always have to deal with scorned women? This woman and I had no connection.

Sam taught me well, she was no match for my skills, just like Halette in Paris, only I hoped for a less morbid outcome. Goose bumps ran up my spine as I remembered the Halette debacle. I unclipped the cord, and spun, forcing my knee between her legs with a vengeance. She crumpled to the floor, and I grabbed the camera a split-second before it hit the floor. I left her there, writhing in pain, clicking the button on the elevator. The doors slid open.

Wasting no time, I bounced in, and hit the big G button. As the doors swooshed closed, I saw her shadow crawling towards me.

The elevator glided to its stop, I tore out the doors, and across the street as if being chased by a psychopath with a bloody knife. La Tige screeched around the corner, and I jumped into the vehicle as we roared off down the street.

"He didn't meet her, but she was there."

"You shouldn't have done that. You coulda got hurt." He said with little emotion as if he precogged I would go chasing after them. "You were good too."

"You watched me!"

"Yup, this business suits you."

"You knew how I would react?"

He drew in a deep breath, "Yup, think it's time you tell me your story?"

He was blunt, and right. A large part of me wanted to talk, but my mouth refused to form the words. "There is no story."

We rode in silence for several minutes until I spoke. "I'll tell you one day, just not yet. What about tonight, the couple?" I changed the subject.

"Fair - I have a story too, but now is not the time either." He said in a firm but gentle voice, the kind I imagined a father would use on his child. "Tell me about tonight?"

No doubt, this entire scenario tonight had been a test, and I passed La Tige detective school 101.

I relayed the evening's events to La Tige. At the office, we downloaded and scanned through the pictures.

Are You Ready for Some Football?

Sunday rolled around, and I forgot my so-called date, although I was about to be rudely reminded. I sat cross legged on the couch relaxing with my Sunday coffee when the doorbell rang. I figured it was the neighbor from the building next door wanting to borrow more sugar, or an egg so I opened the door. To my surprise, Fetch stood before me decked out in a bright red jersey with a giant white number 80 sewn onto the front.

"Good morning Fetch," I didn't try to hide my annoyance.

"I came prepared. I knew you wouldn't have a jersey." He handed me a bag; a smile stretched across his lovely face.

"You brought me a present?"

"Sure, you can't go watch a game without proper attire. This is San Francisco, home to the Forty Niners, five-time Super Bowl champs!" Like I would know.

My mouth opened, but no sound came out. He bought me a jersey, and he looked pathetic, though in a mouth-watering kind of way. With my hands I motioned for him to take a seat on the couch, then I disappeared into my bedroom slipping on the jersey, displaying a large number seven printed on the front, along with a name I dared not pronounce for fear of screwing it up, and a pair of jeans.

The sun shone brilliant in the sky, a couple puffy white clouds dotted the sky, and a slight bay breeze swept over the city. Beyond any doubt one of the most perfect fall days I ever witnessed. On the drive there he opened the sunroof, allowing a constant air current to circulate about the car. With the radio down low we talked. It turned out he was a *freelance* artist/bridge builder and moved to the city as part of the crew that built the new Bay Bridge. He claimed it was good money. He explained the bridge used to be two levels; the lower level flowing into the city of Oakland, and the upper level flowing into San Francisco.

Fetch logic stated, San Francisco had the most amazing views anywhere in the country; therefore, it made sense for the upper level to empty into San Francisco. I didn't know if that was true, but it sounded good and the city did have one of the most amazing skylines I'd seen in my travels. He explained how the Golden Gate got the publicity, but the skyline shots photographers took from the Bay Bridge.

"How do you know all this?" I asked to get a word in edgewise, I never met a man that talked so much, or I'd been spending too much time with La Tige the humpher.

"I'm an artist, building the bridge helped to support my painting career. Mostly scenery like the views from the bridge, but also people. I capture their emotions with brush-strokes." His excitement filled each word.

"Don't most painters choose either scenery or people?" I asked this from my experience in Paris. Didier loved artwork, and it always seemed artists stuck to a single type of artwork.

"I'm not most people. I paint and sketch where my heart is. My apartment is my studio come home with me and I'll show you."

I changed the subject as I didn't want to rush into his apartment today; things might happen as I had an extreme weakness for mouth-watering men, and he piqued my female senses. "How did you know where to find me today?"

He chuckled. "Kacy. I help her out. Something breaks in the bar, she calls me, I fix it, then she credits my tab. My apartment is across the street from Happy Trails."

"You're a handyman too?" Wow! A maintenance man. I went from wealthy beyond measure to a handyman whose dream in life is to become the next Picasso. This relationship was going nowhere. I came up in this world since leaving my beautiful Didier at the altar, NOT!

He sensed my sarcasm because he suddenly became defensive. "It pays my rent and yes when my landlord has a problem in one of the apartments, I fix it."

Smooth, Cleo I thought. He's hot, works hard, and reminded me of my Einstein, a gorgeous, energetic man with work ethics and dreams. Perhaps he reminded me of Einstein too much.

"What about you?"

I knew this was coming. At some point I would be put on the spot - Shanna had no pre-planned past life. Once I began the lie flowed like water. I fabricated a story about my father being in the military, causing us to travel a lot to cover any slip-ups I might make about my travels.

The game was an exhilarating rush of excitement. We started with the tailgaters and the pregame entertainment; bands played on a stage and cheerleaders did a dance of sorts. Fetch did his best to explain football to me: first downs, touchdowns, field goals, sacks. I understood most of it; the rest I just tuned out. I didn't need to catch up on a lifetime of NFL schooling in an entire afternoon.

My voice grew hoarse by the end of the third quarter from yelling at every run, touchdown, and miraculous move they made. I hollered and screamed. The Forty Niners won my heart. The fans were classy, not harassing to the few poor souls who wore jerseys for the opponent. Yet the beer was far too overpriced. If Kacy charged stadium prices for a beer she'd never have any customers. In my case, I wasn't paying for it anyway. San Francisco won.

After the game, Fetch took me out for less expensive beer, and a tour of the city. We stopped in a small, comfy, local bar the size of Happy Trails during karaoke night. I found myself surprised at the number of people with great singing voices, and less surprised at those who attempted to sing but failed miserably, leaving my ears in distress.

A blast of vibrant red hair caught the corner of my eye. My own curiosity caused my full vision to drift towards the redhead, who happened of all things to be the same redhead, Mrs. Nomes, whom I'd blasted with a crotch blow. She appeared caught up in her conversation, which I hoped meant she hadn't spotted me.

My head buried deep in thought I didn't notice Fetch disappear until the music started again and a familiar voice talked over the mic. I looked to the stage and there he was.

"This song is for that lovely lady." His gaze caught mine as the words flowed from his mouth while stretching his hand in my direction. She noticed me now. Her red hair turned into flames of fire and smoke billowed through each ear. I shook the vision out of my head, choosing to ignore her and focus on this mouth-watering man of many shocking talents beyond what he'd mentioned in the car. The words to "Wonderwall" by Oasis flowed off his tongue like honey to my heart. No one ever serenaded me before, unauthorized tears rolled down my cheeks. After the song he took a seat next to me, wiping the tears from my cheeks with his finger.

"That was amazing" I yearned to jump him, but used self-control instead.

He pulled me towards him and we locked in a far too comfortable embrace.

In the year or so I spent in San Francisco, I hadn't enjoyed the nightlife. Tonight, with Fetch, I felt free. I was more and more finding myself. One small but disturbing dilemma stood in my way: who was I really?

Fetch interrupted my thoughts. "You hungry? I know a great place that sells giant burritos."

"Sure." He changed the mood in a matter of seconds; a tender Fetch, to fun loving Fetch.

I winked at Mrs. Nomes on my way out the door as smoke continued to billow from her ears.

"They are giant. I bet you can't eat a whole one," he taunted.

A challenge, I couldn't resist and learned young to eat when opportunity arose, so I cajoled him back. "I may not look like much, but I bet I can eat more than you."

A smirk crawled across his face. "Let's bet. If I eat more than you, you have to go to Santa Cruz with me."

So, he wanted a real bet, no problem! "All right, but if I win you have to drink five of Kacy's Napalm Deaths." He wanted a romantic getaway with me and I chose something sure to burn up his tongue, throat and esophagus, then creep into his gut. Not an equal bet and I felt a little stupid having said it.

He twisted his lips into a devilish smile and jeered, "You're on."

He hadn't exaggerated. One mammoth sized burrito was a meal equivalent to three days' worth.

Halfway through I slowed, each bite became a chore. I forced myself onward. He showed no sign of fullness. Our eyes locked in a bet-you-can't-eat-another-bite stare. My stomach yelled STOP! It begged for me to quit, but I couldn't back down with only a few more bites. He was within a couple bites of finishing as his were much larger than mine. *Stop! Quit!* Begged my guts as I swallowed another bite, and then another. He choked down his last bite, showing signs of being too full, the bite lingered in his mouth, and a grimace took over his face as he swallowed. I took a deep breath and swallowed another bite that threatened to creep up my esophagus. I gathered my will power swallowing the last of my burrito. It went down as easy as eating a rock and dropped to my stomach like one.

Fetch's eyes displayed surprise and admiration. "I'm impressed. I never thought anyone as little as you could eat that much at one time. How did you ever learn to do that?"

Time for another story, telling stories grew old fast, so I gave a half truth. "Like I said earlier my dad was military, and my mom didn't work cause we moved every couple years, so we didn't have much money and there were four of us. We learned to eat the food presented to us, and we cleaned our plates." Burnt out on my own tall tales I changed the subject. "We both won, so what next?"

"Simple, we go to Kacy's and I drink five Napalm Deaths and you go to Santa Cruz with me." A large smile covered his face, and twinkles lit up his silver eyes like fireworks.

At this point my eyelids were heavy and drooping, partly from the monster mammoth burrito settling into my belly and partly because of the day's events and excitement. "Can it wait? I'm really tired."

"Let's get you home. We'll do Santa Cruz when the weather is warm." He said with a smile that almost drove me to plunge my tongue into his adorable mouth.

Before we parted for the night, he planted a kiss on me that elevated me off the ground and into another dimension. My thoughts lingered on the touch of his lips against mine as I fell into a deep sleep that felt more like being under a spell.

No More Lollygagging

Over the next several days I busied myself at work to alleviate my consuming desire for Fetch that led to multiple daydreams, and continue my own search in finding answers to my mysterious birth.

Since I passed La Tige's test he left me alone most days while he spied on Mrs. Nomes and various other clients, which allowed for my own research using his data banks. I started with Frank Tomey. He had quite a rap sheet of varied crimes, everything from holding up quicky-marts to manslaughter - his hit and run that cost me Einstein. His current incarceration of twenty years along with the prison flashed before my eyes. I contemplated paying him a visit. He couldn't hurt me from behind bars, but he may be able to answer questions. I saved that as a last resort.

I correlated his rap sheet to my birth. His first arrest occurred when I was two and a half for petty theft. The charges didn't stick, and they released him back into society. I scanned all his other charges and realized they hardly ever stuck. The courts released him, dropped the charges, or reduced his sentences. That gave me another idea. Who was his lawyer? He always had the same lawyer, Mitchell Strat. Who was Mitchell Strat and how did a lowlife like Tomey have such a great lawyer? Strat had many clients including someone named Briggs, his wealthiest clients. The name Briggs rang bells because the police found a connection between them and Frank Tomey. Maybe the same connection I just found, but that didn't mean they knew each other. I mulled the information over in my head for a few days.

Then I researched the Briggses. They owned a large conglomeration of real estate business offices they rented out across the nation. The Briggses were rich, why share their lawyer with bottom-sucking scum like Tomey? I decided the lawyer must be on the Briggs' payroll. Many of the lawyer's other clients were like Tomey, rap sheets and charges that never stuck. Most of Tomey's crimes occurred in New York. My curiosity piqued and my sixth sense screamed *find the answers in New York*.

La Tige's gruffness interrupted my thoughts of infiltrating the Briggs' conglomerate. I hadn't even heard him come into the office. "Nu, need you again tonight."

Instead of heading home, we headed for parts unknown. He filled in the details during the drive.

"She's a stalker."

"Mrs. Nomes?" She's weird and creepy, but a stalker?

"Been tailing her for weeks. She follows the partner like a puppy dog, only she never talks to him, never." He said it as I expect a trained police officer would, with a profound sense of right and wrong, stalking all wrong.

"That would make sense, but why was she at the hotel and who is the other woman?"

"His wife."

We arrived outside a tall house with views that overlooked the entire city. While waiting we broke into a conversation about his cop days, and he pulled a small, wrinkled, yellowed picture out of his wallet.

It had seen better days. He handed it to me without saying any words. In the palm of my hand lay a picture with corrosion so intense the child on it downright unrecognizable. Perdy's picture. "What... why..." My mouth stumbled, searching for the right words.

"You asked about this case." A sense of 'I know' resounded in his voice.

Tears formed behind my eyes, threatening to drop, and my throat became salty. I choked everything back and played stupid. "A 'waterlogged' picture?"

"Hmm... the woman we found in the river. Until the mysterious phone call this was our only clue."

"Who's in the picture?"

"Her daughter/son?" His intense gaze scanned my eyes, prying for information. Did he recognize me, did he suspect? He couldn't. The picture's damage so extreme I couldn't even make out my face, surely no one else would make the connection.

Mrs. Nomes and her flaming red hair exited the home, and hopped into her convertible that was as red as her head, saving me from further speculation.

We tailed her little red car through the city, over the Golden Gate Bridge, and into

Sausalito. Fetch's words about the Golden Gate getting credit for San Fransisco's amazing skyline rang through my mind and I snuck a glimpse as we exited the city. A tiny smile crossed my lips as I realized the truth in his words. The houses on the Sausalito side were huge, and the area loaded with trees.

Mrs. Flaming Redhead Nomes finally came to a stop and exited her car. She slunk down the street, turning her head every few seconds to confirm nobody was in the area following her. As the camera girl I captured her movements in pictures and zoomed in snapping a few close-ups for giggles. The look on her face was priceless; her eyes bugged out from her face as if someone released suction cups from them. Her buggy eyes bounced back and forth as her hands fumbled with the lock on the door.

"Nu, you come up the front. Don't go in. I'll be going in from the back." He said, laying a heck of a bombshell on me. At that moment I felt proud, like I was actually his partner, no, more than that. Since the day we met a connection formed, something more than friendship, but too unfamiliar yet to be discerned.

I waited at the front door, my back against the house with my ear molded to the siding. I heard an eerie, dead silence, so I slid the door open a smidge, enough to peer inside the home. The lights from the street illuminated a sliver that flowed over the tile floor and rested on a family picture of Mr. Nomes' partner Fred and his wife Jeanne. The suspense wrenched at my guts, and I figured since I opened the door a smidge I might as well slip inside before she noticed the sliver of light. Inside I fumbled around blindly in the darkness with my hands outstretched attempting to avoid bumping into something that would crash and give away my position. My eyes adjusted to the darkness, and a hallway appeared. I tip-toed down the hallway with the utmost caution.

A dim light shone from under a doorway. I drew closer and closer to the light as I eased towards it. From behind, a strong male hand wrapped around my mouth and forced me into him. Not a smart thing to do. I always got caught from behind so my self- defense moves kicked in and I elbowed his ribcage hard. An out of breath La Tige sputtered in a whisper, "Nu, shit."

I returned his whisper, "I'm sorry. I'm so sorry. You freaked me out. It was self-defense."

The siren of a police car flooded my ears and survival mode mixed with memories took control of my body. I ran, taking no caution to the noise I made. By the time I reached the car I realized my error, I left La Tige alone. Logic kicked in and I walked towards the house. The sirens blasted the air around me, and two police officers stepped out of the vehicle. One officer motioned for me to move away from the house while the other walked inside past me.

"You're Nu?" Asked the cop outside, a female with short cropped hair.

Dumbfounded, I expected them to come after me for my past crimes. It dawned on me that I was the good guy in this little scenario.

"Yeah, did La Tige call you?"

She nodded her head 'yes'. Her eyes fixated on the house. The other officer, a man, escorted an angry, cursing Mrs. Nomes in handcuffs. Her eyes like daggers as they fixated on me and another slew of curse words, this time directed towards me, spilled from her mouth like a bad case of the runs.

The officers tucked her into the car. La Tige limped towards me. "That was one hell of an elbow." He shook his head with a smile across his squarish face.

"Be careful, I'll do it again."

"I came out the front door with the evidence I needed. Didn't see you so went back inside the house. Shouldn't have grabbed you from behind." His blue eyes twinkled under the streetlights.

I twisted my mouth into a smile. "What evidence?"

"She poisoned their orange juice. Her fingerprints are all over the carton. I called it in then went looking for you." The smile vanished from his face while his eyes took on a serious intensity. "Why did you run? You knew it was me."

Another story or the truth? I was a professional tale weaver and opted to tell another. "I freaked out. As a kid my friend Burke and I were playing with his puppy, Chops, in the front yard of his house. Chops spotted a cat, the cat ran, and Chops followed along after him. We chased them to the creepy, dilapidated abandoned house on our block. Paint crumbled off the walls, two by fours nailed the door shut, and inside the curtains drooped off their rods. It looked like a haunted movie house. We called Chops, but he wouldn't come. We found a broken window so Burke used my back as a stepping stool to climb through the window.

"After what seemed like forever, he finally reappeared with Chops in his arms. The police rounded the corner, sirens blaring. They made us put our hands up and handcuffed us then stuffed us into the police car. The police took us to the station, Chops too, and called our parents. They didn't arrest us but the owners of the house wanted to press charges for breaking and entering. It was scary!"

La Tige shook his head up and down and humphed his usual humph.

We rode to the police station, made our statements then headed to the office. He placed a key in my hand and curled his gigantic fingers around it swallowing mine. My eyes locked onto his. "Unsolved cases - I hope you find what you're looking for." He turned on his heels and walked out the door.

Unsolved Cases Drawer

umbfounded again. My nose stuffed up, and tears rolled across my cheeks. He gave me the key, my kidnapper-mom Perdy's case. I opened the drawer and pulled out its only contents - two manila folders. I placed them both on my desk. The first was a missing woman. Her emerald eyes jumped off the page at me, her skin dark tan like mine. The longer I stared at her features, the more life-like she became. As I unlatched her photo from the paper clip holding it in place a thought occurred.

I looked in the bathroom mirror and held the picture beside my face. We looked so much alike we could pass for sisters. Was this my biological mother? I ran back to my desk, the folder contained few notes even her name was sketchy, either *Mali or Aaliyah*. A few more sloppy chicken scratched words blotted the page... *disappeared, hospital, after giving birth, child deceased*. I flipped through the rest of the files' contents and found a death certificate. The name of the child was too blurry for me to read, although the date was clear. If this child lived, he or she would be a few years younger than me. I chalked up my physical likeness to the mother as happenchance.

I flipped through the folder and found a balled up then re-straightened newspaper article about the woman from the first photo and her strange disappearance from the hospital. Her husband, a police officer, grieved his missing wife and deceased child. La Tige had been on the force then, so I surmised this had to be one of his fellow cop buddies. My experience with La Tige taught me cops were family.

The second file was on Perdy, the mom who raised me. Her label, *Jane Doe #6*. I read through the file and discovered nothing new. Along with a list containing a handful of individuals with matching partials to the fingerprints lifted off her body. Fingerprints! That never came out before, never in all my research - secrets from the media? I don't know why it shocked me so much. The name Frank Tomey stood out straightaway with the words *possibility, alibi shaky* written next to his name. I knew he was guilty and would prove it. He deserved to spend the rest of his life behind bars, no possibility of parole. I clicked on the computer and it whirred to life as I made a pot of coffee.

He worked as a maintenance supervisor for an apartment building in New York. I read the notes and his long rap sheet. Frank clocked in and out regularly for work during the time frame of her murder, scribbled on the note was *guilty, guilty, guilty!* The words maintenance lapsed my thoughts to Fetch, and I made a personal brain note - *maintenance guy, creepy, can't get serious, run.*

The computer screen came to life, blinking at me. I researched who owned the apartment building, which led me to another person, and another, and another. After several minutes I found what I wanted. The Briggses owned the apartment building where he worked. Slug, as he liked to be called, worked for them. He wasn't a maintenance supervisor, but an employee who did their dirty work. The Briggs' family structure consisted of William II, Carol, and their children William III, Candace and Patrice. William I died years ago and his wife Martha just a couple years ago.

William II had a brother named Clyde, and a sister named Sarah. They were both alive and married with children. The entire family lived in New York.

Slug linked me to this family. *Blackmail.* My kidnapper mother Perdy used me somehow to blackmail the Briggses.

Briggs.

Slug's brother said Frank worked as an enforcer for a wealthy family, but he couldn't remember the name: *Britt or Bridge, Bridd?* Briggs, it was Briggs, and I'd heard the name before, in Paris. Detective Young! He'd found the name associated with Einstein's death. They had the wealth and power, and Slug was a direct connection to them.

The puzzle pieces shifted into place before my eyes. Slug was the Briggs' enforcer, doing their dirty work. Perdy stole me, and Slug was sent to retrieve or execute me. She kept me safe from them. She said so in her letter, which I read a million times and memorized, *They are real rich and could do most anything they want... Don't ever let them find ya.* Whose baby am I? My skin is much darker than any photos of the family I found. A thought lingered at the tip of my mind and swirled into a full-fledged epiphany. I must have belonged to someone who crossed them. That would answer the *why* that bounced off my cranium into the gray matter inside my head. It was a personal or a business vendetta against a formidable opponent of theirs. I needed to get in with this family, find an opening, I needed to get my butt to New York.

The wheels turned at high speed in my brain. I had never before been this close. I spent the next hour typing a résumé, and finding open positions within the Briggs' company infrastructure, I emailed my résumé.

Santa Cruz

"Please join us. We would have such an awesome time. You need a break, Alex's got this, Ka-cy." I pleaded, giving her my biggest puppy dog eyes. I had never before resorted to such tactics; however, I couldn't think of a better time to start. I batted my eyes towards Alex, who did a shrug-chuckle at the same time.

"I got this Kacy. Go, enjoy yourself for one weekend." Alex said in his most assuring tone.

"Begging, Shanna, really? OK, if Javier can make it, we'll go."

"Ahh... Thank you, thank you!" I jumped off my barstool and gave her the biggest hug, wrapping my body around her.

"Shanna, you're cutting off my airflow."

The following day packed and ready we crammed into Fetch's car since this whole thing was his idea. It was a perfect summer day. I had been seeing Fetch for a few months, kinda, since the football game.

Fetch opened up the sunroof allowing the dry summer air to circulate through his car, and we blasted the tunes, sang and took goofy pictures all the way there. Kacy caught me with my tongue out, head tilted to the left, and I captured a pic of her doing a weird eye-roll thing. We stopped for lunch and I clicked one of Fetch and Javier balancing fries on their noses. It was a contest to see who could balance a fry the longest. Fetch won that one.

We arrived in Santa Cruz and stopped at the Boardwalk. I insisted. I never tickled my toes in the Pacific. Before Fetch shifted the car into park, I threw off my shoes and ran like a mad woman towards the ocean, which curved into privatish coves surrounded by beach. The sand felt hot, burning my feet with each pound of my foot, which contrasted when they hit the water by freezing my feet into instant ice cubes. "Shit, the water is cold!" I proclaimed jumping out and running into Fetch, who picked me up and swirled me in circles until we were both dizzy, laughing at my naivete.

We walked the length of the boardwalk. There were rides, shops, machines to drop your money into for games and fortunes. I found myself running everywhere like a child, grabbing Kacy one moment and Fetch the next.

I never rode a roller coaster. Kacy was correct when she suggested I grew up under a rock. Good American-made fun, and I never experienced it. The four of us, with my persistence, rode every thrill ride. I stole Kacy away, insisting she ride with me. I adored Fetch, and that worried me. He was so much like Einstein, only a freer spirit, which Einstein may have been under different circumstances. The problem with having a "relationship" with Fetch is we're both free spirits, and I needed a stable man, not an artist/handyman/bridge builder/dreamer. Someone in a relationship needed to be mature; in ours nobody was. Instead of riding with Fetch, I chose Kacy - my best friend even though she knew nothing of my familial issues. Kacy would always be there.

After a few hours on the Boardwalk I wore everyone out and we retired to the beach house! Nothing Fetch did surprised me, but I was curious how he secured a house on the beach in Santa Cruz.

The look in my eyes gave away my thoughts. "My landlord owns it. He lets me stay here whenever."

"It's amazing."

He unlocked the front doors which opened into a large - massive house. In Paris I lived in a hotel, but never stepped foot into a single-family home this size. I knew my eyes gave my emotions away. Fetch looked at me with his grin and silver bullet eyes, then he picked me up like a baby doll and carried me up the spiral staircase.

He threw me onto the soft padded bed, and laid his firm long body over mine, dropping angel kisses over my chest and abdomen until his lips settled on mine.

After our bed excursion, while laying on my back, Fetch traced an invisible line from my chest to belly button. "Your abs are perfect."

"You think, I walk everywhere." I turned over to lay on my back, he continued tracing his finger across my flesh, the length of my spine, across the small of my back and up again.

"I've never met anyone as perfect as you." He rested his head on my back, tufts of his long dark hair lay limply across it.

Within minutes he fell asleep his warm breath teasing the skin on my back, and my thoughts wandered.

Fetch and I weren't a "thing". At least the term relationship never came up in discussion. We saw each other once or twice a week, hung out, enjoyed each other and cooking. Sometimes we cooked together, he was competitive and I couldn't resist the chances to one-up him at something, so we devised cooking contests, using Kacy's customers as judges. It turned out our skills were equal.

Fetch's apartment was a typical bachelor pad - a mess. His clothes lay in haphazard piles across his couch, chairs, and floor. His TV was the size of a movie screen, and he wouldn't allow anyone but him to touch his prized remote. A stack of 'girlie magazines' formed a mountain beside his bed. My first visit I noticed the swimsuit calendar, the one I modeled in, at the top of the mountain. He stepped into the kitchen, I snatched the calendar and stuffed it into my oversized purse. Paranoid maybe, careful definitely. As an artist, he had an eye for detail, and would notice me, as Justine, in a heartbeat.

His studio was a nook, the only part of his apartment he kept organized. Paintings, and sketches covered every inch. In the last few months I became the subject of his art. He filled an entire sketchpad of me sleeping, turning, and stretching. I flipped through the pad and the scenes played as a movie. Lost in my thoughts, I too fell asleep, awaking when the warm spot on my back turned cold from Fetch lifting his head. I opened my eyes to his silver bullets caressing every centimeter and curve of my body. *Am I in love with him?*

For dinner the four of us ordered a pizza and spent the night basking in the hot tub, drinking Kacy's Napalm Death. The bet was Fetch would drink five, and he did, consecutively. We all drank one or two.

"While you're up, I can barely hear the music," hollered Kacy towards a stumbling Fetch.

"Music... uh... yeah."

I found it necessary to maneuver Fetch towards the restroom and myself to the radio which I had trouble figuring out how to work. Lucky for me there was a remote attached, which I handed to Javier as I sank into the hot tub.

Fetch wandered into the room a few minutes later, walking sideways and stumbling as he made his way back to the hot tub in time for what Javier called a Mini-Rita. Fetch immersed himself into the hot tub next to me, slurring his words, "I likethat sssuit, butIthink you wouldbe prettieroff." The look on his face was classic. His lips turned up in a devious smile, and his silver bullets shone bright with flecks of blue and green dancing in them. We drank the Mini-Ritas, except Fetch; he reached his limits hours earlier. With Javier at the music helm, he found fantastic dance music. I took Kacy's hand, and we danced right out of the hot tub and across the patio. It felt better than the day I met Fetch.

The night drew to a close as Fetch fell asleep in the hot tub. With Javier and Kacy's help we escorted him to the wide pillow-fluffy couch.

"I'll get him by the arms and lift, you girls grab his feet." Javier ordered.

"He weighs a ton." Kacy expressed as she grabbed his right leg. I grabbed his left, which distributed his weight more evenly.

"On the count of three toss him to the couch, one… two…"

"Stop! I can't toss him. What if he hits the floor instead? I think we should get closer." I suggested, imagining his back hitting and bouncing off the side of the sofa.

We moved a couple steps closer and heave-hoed him smack in the center of the puffy couch where he grabbed hold of my bikini bottoms, forcing me off balance so I fell onto him. He curled his arms around me and we both fell into a deep sleep.

The rest of the weekend we roamed the beach, the Boardwalk, and ordered various dishes, sampling each others'. At times we moved as an entire four-person young adult not-a-care-in-the-world group and at other times we split off to shop, ride the coasters, or tan. There were few moments in my life that stuck out as memorable in a fantastic way; my first movie with Einstein, beach day in Aruba with the girls, Didier's proposal on the French Riviera, and this weekend. It would live high on a pedestal.

Seeking Truths

It took a few months, but I got the call from New York, and accepted a position as a secretary, low on the totem pole at Briggs International. The only people I informed were Kacy, whom I paid the entire month's rent, and La Tige when I gave my two weeks. La Tige already knew and wrote an eloquent, glowing recommendation. He didn't write it himself.

I refused telling Fetch and asked Kacy not to give him my address when I found a place in New York. He weighed heavy on my mind and whether I was making the correct decision. I didn't know the answer. He never confessed love to me or I to him. It was more of a physical, primal attraction with a boatload of good times attached. Kacy was always one to express her thoughts, never holding back, and felt I was making a huge mistake. Her words were, 'Shanna that man, whether he knows it or not, is madly in love with you. OMG, you two are so perfect for each other! Mark my words, he'll find you, you're like kindred spirits or something.' If we were kindred spirits then we wouldn't be able to stop love from happening one day.

La Tige drove me to the airport where he shared a few more surprises for me. As we drove to the drop-off area, he pulled his beast-vehicle over and unloaded my bags for me, then he wrapped his arms around me, and gave me a squeeze. It was that gesture, that moment that made me realize the connection between us; he was a father figure to me. Without words, we both cried, my tears streaked down my face while his lingered at the corners of his eyes.

"Nu, you always have a job here." Earlier I returned the phone he gave me when I started working for him. He handed it back. "Keep the phone, use it to call or text whenever you need, anything you need."

Call? He disliked talking on the phone, much preferring texting. "Thank you." I blubbered through my tears.

I saw a tear crawl from the corner of his eye as he turned to leave. He climbed into his vehicle and I watched his car pull out and roar down the road. He preferred I didn't catch him crying. La Tige, always the tough man.

After I checked my bags, made the uncomfortable trek through security, and found my gate, I took a seat to wait it out. I pulled the phone out of my purse, ran my finger along its sleek edge remembering many good times then flipped it open, and found a note inside, which I unfolded. It read:

Call this number when you get to NY 555-6783. Rent controlled apartment.

Find your answers.

La Tige

Bite the Big Apple
Baby Girl Book IV

Miss Executive
Secretary

A few drops of wine swirled in the bottom of my glass. I tapped my phone's speaker icon to free my hands and refill the glass. Kacy's voice filled my small rent-controlled studio apartment - a tip from La Tige, my ex-boss and father figure in my life...

"Girlie, how'd you land this fantastic new job?" Kacy and I spoke once a week, sometimes more. I found it refreshing to keep a friend while at the same time disturbing. I never kept relationships of any kind, except James.

"His bulldog of a wife, she looks like a bulldog, jaw jowls, bent arms, the whole works. It met her during the annual Christmas party. She walked inside at the same time I walked outside for fresh air.

The night air was warm for December in New York. She slammed into me and I flew backwards into the trash can. Thank God it was lidded or I would've been sitting in it."

"She didn't! I woulda kicked her bulldog…"

"I'm not done. She scowled on the way inside, never turning her head mind you, 'I hope that orange mop isn't natural, you're a disgrace to the company'".

"I totally woulda chased her down and whooped on that rich bully ass." The tension in her voice obvious.

"I'm sure you would have, but I'm classier than that."

"Whatever! Miss-I-left-my-boyfriend without sayin' a word." I heard Kacy chuckling on the other end and detected a slight hesitation in her voice.

"You told him, didn't you?" My voice laced with angst over a man who wasn't my boyfriend. At least we never voiced the words. Fetch was a play guy, simmering hot, but no life goals. I refilled my wine glass again and allowed the sweet red juice to drizzle down my throat.

"I didn't… You got me, I did. But only that you took a better job in New York. I didn't give him your address or anything."

"Some best friend you are!" The two times Fetch called I ignored the rings, allowing the calls to go to voice mail, but he left none.

"He's like the hottest guy ever. He comes into the bar like a broken puppy, droopy eyes, no spark. I'm a sucker for puppies and I told." Kacy was a sucker sometimes, but she hadn't watched a boyfriend, my Einstein, get jolted across the road during a hit and run and die in front of her eyes or stood her next lover, Didier, up on the altar because she pretended to be something she wasn't. No, that was me. A broken home led to my broken life which I desperately tried to fix.

"I'd kick your butt if I was there."

Silence filled the air for thirty seconds before Kacy replied.

"Sorry sweet. I think he's in love with you. The two of you make the best couple I've ever seen."

"I know and I'm not angry. I... He never said the words. If I'm meant to be with Fetch It'll work Its way out, somehow, someday. If not, then we aren't meant for each other."

"You are a romantic fool. Sometimes you gotta take life by the horns and just do it." Sentiment crawled into each of Kacy's words.

Desperate to get off the Fetch topic I rerouted the conversation. "After bulldog slammed into me, William III unplastered me from the trash can. We talked. Would you believe his parents refused to let him watch movies like the Wizard of Oz or Oliver Twist when he was a kid?"

"No freakin' way!" The volume of her voice almost burst my ear drums.

"Yes freakin' way, according to him his parents said those movies were too scary and would give him nightmares. Instead, his parents forced him to watch the news or the stock market."

"No Sesame Street?"

"None! I'm surprised he turned out so normal." Not that I watched Sesame Street either but I wished I had.

"My mind is blown. Poor deprived children. How many kids are there again?"

"William III is the oldest Briggs child, then Patrice and last Candace."

"I'm shocked they made it to adulthood." We both chuckled at her response. "Keep going babe, wanna hear the rest."

"I went home and Monday, when I arrived at work, I had an email from him to meet at Vinny's New York Style Brick Oven Pizza House. He sent directions.

"An unhappily married man wanting lunch with a receptionist. All kinds of thoughts and images went through my mind."

"Creeepy."

"Exactly. OK, we met for lunch. I was tense and ready to run thinking affair no way! Turns out he asked me to be his executive secretary. You already know I accepted. The best part, my pay has tripled!"

"Luck finds you. Got no complaints. Love my bar, my bar is my life. No, that's not true - Javier is my life."

"Incorrect, the bar is your life, Javier is secondary." The chilly air brought scents of various cuisines into my apartment through the open sliver of my window. They mingled with the garlic smell from the Italian chicken I cooked for dinner.

"He is not. He's busy with school all the time and the bar... I love the bar, the people... its home." She meant that as she grew up above the bar. During the time we lived together, I saw similarities in our lives, although hers was a lot more normal than mine. I lived in a shack with a junkie fake mom who went missing and turned up dead floating in the Bay just beyond the mouth of the Sacramento River. That life did a number on me and pushed me to grow up long before my time. Kacy grew up above a bar with a happy family, even so she grew up quick.

"You're hopeless. Javier will marry you one day and the two of you will stroll off into the wild blue yonder together, forgetting the rest of us."

"So not true. My bar will be the milk and bread of our marriage if it ever happens. At least until he gets a job that pays enough, and we can raise a family. And you'll be the Maid of Honor at our wedding."

"Who is the hopeless romantic now?" I recognized how much she adored every millimeter of Javier.

"I totally love you Shanna." My body cringed at that name, not that I hadn't gotten used to it but I wanted to be me, Cleo. Not Shanna or Justine or even my mom's name for me, but Cleo - short for Cleopatra, as Einstein put it. I needed to face facts - I would always love the one I

could never have. Slug ruined his life, our
life. My love whom one day I would meet
again if there was a heaven. I desired to tell
Kacy everything. She was my best friend,
only I didn't understand the entire story
yet. What would I say? At this point I
understood the Briggs' hired Slug as a 'hit
man' and my kidnapper-fake-mom-junkie
Perdy stole me to protect me from evil
powerful people who hunted me.

"Kacy, you are the best friend ever."
And one day I will tell you the entire story.

Meet the Briggses

Since coming to New York, I changed my appearance choosing to be careful, more than ever, as my enemies lived close. To disguise my eye color, I wore brown contacts. I paid a visit to a salon, and the beautician colored my hair a less obnoxious shade of orangey-yellow. I added fake nails and wore plenty of makeup. Between the makeup and nails I looked the part.

I got much better insight to the entire Briggs family working for William III - he preferred Will. He was a thirty something good-looking, small built man with light blond thinning on top hair. He stood 5'9, maybe 5'10, slim, with fine features. His hazel eyes like a mood ring changed from brown to green. Green meant happy, carefree, and brown meant stress, trouble.

His wife stopped by the office and called millions of times every day. He asked me to lie and use the 'he's in a meeting or with a client' excuses. She was always rude and muttered ugly comments about me under her breath as she hung up the phone.

He spent his days in his office with the door closed. I wasn't sure what he did but his office stayed quiet and people didn't come and go very often. I figured he earned the position in the family business because he was family. His job consisted of nothing, and he spent his work time sleeping. After all, there wasn't anything for him to do because I did everything.

His wife's build and face reminded me of a bulldog. They were an unlikely couple with no children. I thought children might give her something to do rather than harass him 24/7. She stayed involved in charities and fundraisers, the country club, everything rich people do; somehow though, she didn't stay busy enough. I liked Will, but I didn't like his wife. Hate would be too strong a word to describe my dislike for her but disgust fit.

Six weeks after accepting my new position I experienced the family. Will invited me to their beach mansion in the Hamptons for a family/business weekend. First I met William II, Will's father, he was retirement age, 65 or so. His scalp bald on top, with wisps of dark hair framing his head. Unlike his son he had a large build. Like Will his hazel eyes displayed his moods. He could be gruff but well-mannered in social activities; intelligent, controlling and demanding. Nobody crossed him instead they treated him with respect.

Daddy William II's wife, Carol, was petite and quiet, but professional and all business. Candace, Will's youngest sister, didn't get involved in the family business. She spent her time cavorting with Will's wife, planning and plotting social activities. Candace stood tall like her father but otherwise looked much like her mom. Her husband was a lawyer who worked for Mitchell Strat, the lawyer who always got Slug, Einstein's killer, off the hook. I wondered if she knew what a scum sucking pig her husband worked for?

Patrice took after William II, in a non-married female form, cunning, manipulative and meticulous. No doubt her IQ shot above the 130 plus range. She wanted the business and planned on running it like her dad - without scruples. She wore short, dark hair in a boy cut. Her build petite and her glare equivalent to my body being sawed in two pieces with a dull blade. I saw a resemblance in me to Patrice and William II - cunning and meticulous, minus the nasty attitude.

I did the job Will paid me for and observed the behavior of his dysfunctional, powerful, rich family. Like a scientist I studied them analyzing the results and concluded I liked Will, but not the rest of the family. He treated others with respect, including his disgruntled bulldog wife.

As much as possible I stole away from the mansion and walked the million-dollar-home beach. Will stayed occupied with his father and Patrice. After dinner the final night while I sat alone on a designer beach recliner listening to the waves William II joined me without an invitation.

"Beautiful isn't it? My children used to run in and out of the tide right here." His eyes gazed upon the vast ocean before us.

"Lucky kids."

"What about you? What's your story?" Wisps of his thin hair blew over the top of his bald head.

I assumed he was prying more than making conversation. I didn't feel up to another story and wished he leave. His presence ruined the serenity the beach offered. "Don't have one. Normal girl, normal life."

"Everyone has a story."

I smiled and sucked in a deep breath of fresh air. "It'd bore you." To heck if I was going to make up another story to feed his meddlesome curiosity.

"You're the first secretary William's had that is capable of the job."

A compliment? "Thank you, Will… William is easy to work for."

He raised his eyebrows and opened his mouth to continue the conversation when my phone rang. I swiped the talk button. "Hey sis, hold on one second."

I slid my phone away from my ear and apologized to Mr. Briggs. "My sister, I gotta go. Thanks for the weekend. Your home is gorgeous."

He munched his eyebrows into a V and punched his lips together as if upset by my actions. I figured not many people walked away from him.

"Kacy, I'm back."

"Did I hear thanks for the weekend? You have a beautiful house. New guy?"

"No! My boss's father. Will brought me to the beach house this weekend for their

annual family/business get-together..."
Saved by Kacy.

R. T. P Burke Childrone A. K.A. Einstein

I visited Einstein or rather his burial spot. On Sunday mornings, when everyone else went to church, I spent time with Einstein. Sometimes, I sat beside his grave and cried. I missed the chance to grieve his being taken from me by the ugly monster Slug (Frank Tomey). One Sunday I didn't make it until late in the afternoon and his family was there. Or at least I suspected it was his family. The man and woman looked like older versions of Einstein. I saw them and sat on a bench a few feet away. They brought flowers and laid them on his grave. After a long time, they left. I finished my weekly visit and grabbed a coffee. I came by more often hoping to one day build up the courage to speak. On the day I least expected while visiting during the week, after work, I sat beside his grave deep in thought when a voice startled me out of my Einstein reverie.

"Were you friends with my son?" I looked up from my solace to see his mother. Her hair the same shade of blond as Einstein's only with streaks of white. The skin around her gentle eyes bore webs in the creases. She too was tall and thin. He looked much like her.

"No, we never met, but I heard what happened. I think it... is heartbreaking... what happened. I had a friend who... I just wanted to visit and pay my respects." My brain screamed to tell her 'yes, I loved your son' but I couldn't force my mouth to form the words. Instead, I spun another tale.

"My son was a very special young man. He wanted to do incredible things." *He did something incredible*. Einstein loved and took care of me, but I didn't say that.

"Do you mind me asking...? Why he ran?" The questions streamed out of my mouth like water from a hose. I kicked myself mentally for being so insensitive.

"That is not your business." The pain in her eyes evident, although she didn't ask me to leave. Maybe she needed to talk about it, wanted to talk about it. Every day my heart yearned for Einstein and I needed to talk about it and didn't want her running off so I continued.

"I'm sorry. I had a friend who ran and I don't understand why kids leave a good home. You seem like such a nice woman, a good mother. My friend had a good family but still he ran."

I breathed a silent sigh of relief when she continued. "It seems ridiculous now. I can't forgive myself. We didn't always see eye to eye with Burke." For a long time, we stood there, saying nothing, each of us deep in our own sorrow for the same lost young man.

The silence ended when she spoke. "His dreams that didn't fit our plan, our goals for him. We mapped out his life. He couldn't make a move without us. He dreamed of joining the FBI but we refused to let him follow those dreams. Instead we have a business and planned it on passing to him. I guess we tried to control his life too much." Tears rolled down her cheeks, and I held her in my arms. At that moment I felt closer to her than I ever felt to Perdy. We stood there for what seemed like an eternity but in reality, not more than a couple of minutes. He'd never mentioned he wanted to join the FBI. Einstein and I didn't discuss our past lives only our current and future lives. Our dreams squashed by Slug.

She regained composure and said, "Thank-you. I needed that."

"Would you like to join me for some coffee? Latte Latte is just two blocks south?"

She narrowed her eyes, as if deciphering whether to trust me. "Yes, yes. My treat."

We walked to the coffee shop and talked. I told her about my friend, Einstein, and she told me about Burke. We were two women grieving over the same unforgettable young man - my secret. My time spent with Mrs. Childrone gave me closure. His family wasn't the nightmare family I thought they were. They made a mistake and had to live with it much like my mom, Perdy's, mother Leila.

I needed my encounter with Mrs. Childrone. The mystery of my existence wasn't the only one in my life. I always wondered about his family and pictured them with drawn in frowny lips, hate filled eyes, and nasty demeanors. His mother's sweet personality and motherly face gave me answers to at least one of my life's stories. Mr. and Mrs. Childrone owned a large publishing house. She offered me a card, when we parted and on it she wrote her personal email.

www.ingramcontent.com/pod-product-compliance
Lightning Source LLC
Chambersburg PA
CBHW050542190726
48284CB00003B/1184